for Patricia and Michael Green

HALLELUJAH NOW

TERENCE DAVIES

Brilliance Books

First published by Brilliance Books 1984
Copyright © Terence Davies 1984
Brilliance Books 14 Clerkenwell Green London EC1
England

Typeset by MC Typeset of Chatham Kent
Printed and bound in Great Britain by Nene Litho and
Woolnough Bookbinding both of Wellingborough
Northants

ISBN: 0 946189 31 5 Hardback
ISBN: 0 946189 36 6 Paperback

CONTENTS

Part One
Songs for Dead Children 3

Part Two
Letters to a Friend 47

Part Three
The Walk to the Paradise Garden 129

Part One
SONGS FOR DEAD CHILDREN

It's cold this morning, really cold. Dry and misty and breath dissolving on blue-grey, ornate iron railings near the park. Lots of chimneys hidden by the mist, and television aerials quivering in the moist, chilly air.

The kids walk gingerly to school.

Past the bread shop where they sold you flaking barmcakes last summer, past the chemists where the sumptuous yellow light floods out over the paving stones and advertisements about gripe water, with a jolly baby smiling under thin, whisked-up blonde hair, and mothers in red clapping their cigarette-filled hands together for warmth.

One kid walks nervously to school.

Streets stretch from main road to main road with drops of rain shining on bay windows, and rotten wooden eaves over the corner shop dripping in the clean air. Men on their way to work bang doors shut, and the faces of wives at windows touch curtains, then disappear behind still draperies.

When you grow up you might be a king among men.

And oh mummy this is where all the heartbreaks begin, and mummy I want to cry, and steal the wooden counters from Miss Allen's classroom, and forget my lines in the Christmas Play.

A car in Empress Road covered with a canvas. Snugasbuginarug. Toast smothered in butter. Teacups clinking under bright eight o'clock electric lights. Tea with sterilised milk and two sugars. And Christmas in the air.

Mummy what'll Santa bring me for Christmas?

Happy at the thought of so much snow. Happy at the thought of so much happiness.

Yet this mother doesn't answer. Choked with sentiment and love her eyes sparkling but the rims red and sad. She walks with a peculiar roll he'll remember long after this morning has been forgotten, long after its sharp edges have blunted. Her long arms, her skin which bruises easily, her chubby soft hands holding his and smelling of washing soap, and the sound of his new brown shoes tapping tattoos nervously along the pavement.

Don't step on the cracks or black lines – it's bad luck.

Oh lad! Oh son!

And the lump-in-the-throat.

Sun's getting a little stronger but still watery, still trickling down over the rooftops and trees . . . Grovers Corners . . .

Years from now caterpillars will chew leaves and you'll carry home old exercise books and paintings at the end of term. And there'll be adventure in the mist and drama in the rain and thrills in lightning or thunder rolling over like God's indigestion; and during long Indian summers you'll smell the grass and feel akin to the earth; all the days of your life; all that can happen in a thousand years.

And so they walk to school, this Madonna and Child.

A first school day, a barrage of new emotions, a cathartic experience to be treasured or pressed onto the backs of photographs which will fill a handbag in this mother's later, dream-filled years, lying there among the pungent sheets with her snapshots around her (and beneath her, in the living room, her son, smouldering, drinks his cocoa), she'll lie in the room and think and scratch her pink scalp and snore, then sleep, and her hard working hands will lie along the eiderdown and her ungrateful son will look at her as he puts the clock down on the bedside table, and ache to be young again, just to feel those arms around him.

Love me! Love me! Love me! Say you do. Oh mummy protect me! Say the magic word, use the magic wand, take me into the enchanted wood or lead me out of this one.

The iron railings of the school playground. Gleaming in the late autumn sunshine. High in the undecorated facade a plaque commemorating the founder of the school but it's so high up no one can read it. It's in sandstone and weathered away to nothing.

Mummy tell me the legend of the almond tree.

Mummy tell me the saga of the frog pond.

Jump to the sound of whistles in spinsters' mouths, be afraid of the exquisite sadism of brogues on games day. The masochism of the young. The endless boredom of recorded fact. The cosy complacency of religion accepted without question, safe in the knowledge that *God is Love*, that there is no anguish, no decay, then years later learn with agony the tragedy of those lies and watch all your certainties crumble and that there is no Father Christmas, no reindeers in snow-filled skies and certainly no good-will. So enjoy the clinking of glasses, enjoy your street games, let the big ship sail, call in your *very* best friend, imagine yourself to be Huckleberry Finn, yes, enjoy yourself lad it's later than you think.

And so the Madonna and Child walk to school, walking through the yellow autumnal sunlight, walking through the last traces of mist, walking through the crisp leaves of burnished gold and brown. Inside the school spinsters' brogues drumming down a corridor, inside the school, the blackness of nuns – the swish of their habits, the rattle of rosary beads and a wooden crucifix frayed at the edges through so much handling, inside the school, prayers from every classroom echoing into the empty green corridors, inside the school, catechism, the extreme unction to the dying, plenary indulgences if you pray to the Virgin Mary on her feast day in May.

Jesus thou art coming, holy as thou art.

Yellow paracletes, Ave-Ave-Ave-Mar-ri-a, a shilling when you make your first holy communion in a stiff new suit.

Thou who art called the paraclete - Finger of God's right hand.

You'll learn that in Miss Walshes and you'll try to imagine God's hand with a dove-finger but you'll only manage to think of bread, in the shape of corn eaves, standing beneath a Protestant altar at Harvest Festival. Oh the paganism of it! De Profundis, De Profundis, Gluttony in Hell, Magic in Heaven, Feudal systems on a wall, Pear Trees – and the intoxication of a boy! When I was five.

When I was five, when I was five and yes – despite everything – innocent, uncorrupt. After my fifth year there are no more birthdays, only numbers, only pages on a wall.

'Come on! Get up lad.'

And lying in bed wondering why the sheets feel so different today.

'Come on! Lad it's nearly seven o'clock!'

Moving over to get out of bed, his pyjamas feel wet, a wetness confined to a small circle just under the waist – about the size of a half-crown. How did it get there? What is it? Standing in this still, distempered room with the smell of toast for breakfast, tantalizing on a hot plate on the hearth, Down the stairs wondering . . . What could it be? As I draw the green curtain, which serves as a door, the parlour is all radiance. The toast, the melting butter, the fire, the bowl of hot water, the drawn willow-pattern curtains, a china cup so thin you can see the level of your tea – and the odour of that small piece of pus drying on your skin just below the waistline.

Mum smiling in this golden room. 'The' are lad.' Cupping my face with her soft, soft hands. Mummy disappearing through the faded velvet of the green curtain, drooping in folds towards the linoleum.

Plunging my hands into the bowl of water, dissolving the soap, making the water milky blue, washing furiously in the melting light before my mum gets back. Washed. Dried. Ready for inspection. Mother appears exactly on cue and gives me the once over. And again she smiles. A smile which has the power to heal, and cure, and make you feel whole.

'Now eat your breakfast.' Tea gurgling from a pot, ashes shaken with a poker Kevin made at work from spare metal, pressing my stockinged feet against the tiles of the hearth and feeling the warmth creep through the grey wool. The clock strikes eight-thirty and I've got to go to school in a minute. I put on my shoes, my scarf, my coat, my cap. This is it. This is it.

Mother draws the curtains back and the harsh grey light makes everything seem so ordinary, so unpeculiar. How did that pus get there mum? How? She buttons my mac for me and kisses me on the cheek and keeping my face cupped in her hands she says, 'You'll soon be grown up lad.'

Wanting to hold her and never let her go.

'Tara mum.'

And down the steps and into the street.

I look back and she waves, and waves, and smiles, until she is no more than a dot, a mere symbol at a door.

Trailing hands along iron parapet railings, wiping the rust off fingers onto shorts, kicking a stone, running two blocks for no reason at all, looking in sweet shops, putting school-money into the lavender-smelling hands of school-mistresses – the rituals of boyhood – climbing, skipping, warring, playing, artful, crafty, selfish, generous, calling, listening, scuffing, jumping, bashful, spiteful, wilful – the rituals of boyhood.

'Don't go in yet Les. Don't go in – not *just* yet'; let's sit here on the doorstep watching tangerine-white clouds moving across the sky, listening to the wind curling across the waste ground opposite, and a moon. Someone's whistling. 'And if you shine your torch up into the sky the light from it will go on for ever and ever.'

'Just try and count the stars,' – you can't in a sky like that – straight out of your old Eagle annual; escapades at night in Cornwall with the Famous Five or precocious schoolboys getting out of their dorms by shinning down knotted bedclothes then roaming around medieval schoolgrounds, looking for adventure.

'Remember that time we stood looking at that man and woman in that entry and the woman said, "D'you want the left-overs?" Remember?' – and you used to like to go down that entry which led to Phythian Street because you said that the woman in the last house liked to throw her contraceptives over the backyard wall.

Isn't that moon marvellous?

'Don't you go in yet, Les – not just yet.' Let's sit here on the step, beside the railings, and listen to them singing outside the pub at the top of the street.

'When they come down – thee'll be a do.' They'll bring crates, 'a few jars', they'll come in, put the gram on loud so that you can hear the music and dance to it in the street in couples when our parlour has got too hot. 'Later on I'll lie on the sofa – when it gets late – and you feel tired.' When the eyelids droop as you lie behind two people. But you can't go to sleep on the settee, 'cos the magic will be lost for another week, till the next do . . .

'Leslie! Leslie!'

'Hide, Les, hide!'

But Les's dad sees him; Les is summoned from behind the

rotting orange coloured door and in he goes.

The boy sits there on the step, his new torch shining into the great night sky, into the stars you can't count, moonraking. There was a great force moving beneath everything – that boy, on that step, with that torch – was part ot it. There was no one else in the world except him, nothing more important to him except that his friend Leslie should be allowed to sit with him until his family came back from the pub. And behind him that big, Victorian house with its top floor decayed, its disused cellars – a tattered grandeur. Yet he didn't see it. He just kept trying to count stars and listening to the wind across the waste ground, and smelling the wood which supported the railings, and counting marbles in a bag and craving to be grown-up. After many years he would look back on this night, not because anything specific had happened, but because it would symbolize for him the end of childhood, a swan-song for his youth, the apotheosis of happiness. He would never forget it or its perfectness, the air growing still then hot, voices far above the world – singing, that torch, heaven twinkling like a star chamber. And above all an absolute belief that life was going to be one great long adventure and that he would never die. Life was tantalizing, the future glowing with mystery. Soon he'd be grown-up and ahead of him lay adventure, immortality, and great expectations.

I had forgotten Fridays. Wage packets, turbans, girls in factories, lads in wellingtons, cement-filled trousers, bits of cotton, marking chalk, the Overlock, the Buttonhole, white bread tasting of soda, bags of tea, cascades of cakes, ironing on the table, flat irons sizzling on pants, singeing hair. The rush and thump of bodies, cleansing milk, strip washes in the bedroom over the bowl – chipped and wrecked and leaking (the bleeder!), more money than you'd ever seen, hunting for socks, for blouses, for shirts, for small lady like handkerchieves with embroidered flowers on their corners . . . lost.

And their silky skin – my sisters. Their smiling embarassment – my brothers – and an early gathering darkness and the lights sparkling in the early dusk – and out they go – to Ma Shaw's for a drink then at eleven The Loc or The Grafton to jive ferociously and meet a dreamboat, or a seaman, or – get this! – a *Yank*.

And the boys. Initiated into the mysteries of drinking the pint and the humiliations of being turned down for dances. But it didn't matter. After enough beer, after many, many refusals, a kind of smug bravado sets in and your bruised ego forgets that the girl you take home will stand you up outside the pictures on Sunday night, and forgets that her friend is laughing at you and saying loudly under her breath 'Get rid of him!' but only remembers the feeling of those first intoxications, the Dutch courage, the friendships that will never die, the singing and the endless pissing against walls – lost.

Lost – all those grey/sunny Sundays on beaches watching the young men waddle down to the sea. Gone – the sinking into the soft warm sand, watching the sea shimmer and glitter as the sun sank. The last sandwiches eaten, the last of the cream soda frothing at the bottom of the bottle, an egg salad when you got home, warmth in the parlour. Mum calling to the girls, 'Eileen! Maisie! Helen!' as she washed the salad. And after the girls had gone spinning out to their boyfriends, Mum clearing away their lipstick and mascara then dozing in front of the fire as she read the Empire News. And looking at her from across the room as she sighs in her sleep, her coral hands resting on her pinny which smells of rice pudding and flour, wondering what she'll buy me for Christmas. Keeping vigil, lying on the sofa listening to the rain outside and a huge fire curling up the chimney breast.

Is it possible to be so happy?

Is it possible to love her so much?

John and Kevin will come in later and play darts then tease

me at Ludo, the gas will go and they'll file a ha'penny down and put it in the meter then they'll yawn and tumble into bed singing and laughing into sleep. Tony limping home from the docks on his tubercular legs. Then the girls will come in giggling in a posse, leaving kisses at the door. The cocoa made, the toast eaten, mum begins to clear the debris away. 'I'll leave the place till morning,' she says as the last dish drips. 'Come on lad, up the dancers!' With a tired smile. And she bolts the door, switches off the lights and climbs the stairs.

Oh I get the blues when its ray-ay-ayn-in . . . , as she comes up the stairs in the darkness her singing gentle as a caress . . . *The Blues I can't lose when it rains.*

And into bed, and no light, and the rain falls, and the girls dream of legends and princes and the glamour of Crawford, and the lads toss and curse in the wetness of dreams, and I make wish after wish, and still the rain falls.

Do you remember? Do you? Do you remember the first cigarette? The first kiss? The first girl? The first time you saw a woman – *really* saw her – and got that peculiar knot? Like the first shave, like the first close shave – oh you know, her name was Barbara or Aggie and you fumbled your way through the tram ride and ran through the sand and spilt the lemonade.

I want you to try to remember how it was to have felt then, long ago. We will study the Golden Age. We will do homage to The Dream. I want you to remember your first job and how you still let your mam dress you – as if you were still at school – and you left the house extra-early so as not to be late on your first day. Standing outside that office in your blue school mac shivering with nerves. Do you remember sitting down in a corner sick and eager to get on in the world? Can you forget your first week's wages and coming home and giving your mam thirty bob? Can you forget the city lights, your first rush hour, your brushes with lift men, your first tea break, your first argument and all that blushing?

Can you, will you ever forget?

Can you forget the salmon and cucumber sandwiches on brown bread for the office manager? Can you forget the crushed barm-cakes and weeping boiled ham pushed into your mac pocket in a brown folded paper bag? Can you forget the bills of lading and the big wainscoted paying desks of Ellerman and Papayanni Lines and the vast Indian reception hall of Elder Dempster? Can you forget adding up the stamp book and running out of envelopes?

Can you, will you ever forget?

Do you remember the men who seemed to have so much power and the women with big hearts? Do you remember the lady who read G.K. Chesterton, who sprinkled herself with lavender water, who argued with gentility and who with a slight turn of the head, a smallish phrase, could rip you open with a genteel insult? Do you remember the heads of departments, men with glasses and no hair, who wielded magic, enchanted words – *mortage* and *freehold* – and who 'served' the company for twenty-five grudging years?

Can you, will you always remember?

And after the first one, a tumble of jobs, a stretch of careers reaching back as far as the eye can see, but won't look.

Shivering at the bus stop under frail yellow sunlight. Standing on the platform not wanting to get off. Hoping that this ride, this bus journey could last for ever. Cars coming in from the suburbs with mist on their roofs – gleaming, sweating, residential things. Ambition tumbles down leaving you exposed like raw meat on a slab. Naked and vulnerable.

'Adventure has gone out of my life,' he thought. 'Getting pompous too!'

And a million preoccupations – quarters figures are due, mustn't be late again, that'll make twice this week, it's not my job to help with sales, oh my arse on it! What have I done with my life? What have I done with my time? I've just kept changing jobs. If I can just keep that little spark inside me alive and remain interesting I'll be alright. Chances are I might settle down, chances are I might be happy – but then chance would be a fine thing.

'I knew someone who died like that.'

'What?' Still in a world of my own.

'I said I knew someone who died like that.' The bus conductor shouting at me as all the passengers have to squeeze past me in order to get off.

'Oh' I said, and got off.

'Soft bastard!' he shouted after me.

And I walked down to catch the ferry, and God it's cold.

Pigeons cooing in the grain silos, crying overhead then dipping towards the waves or squabbling for food. Cooing like doves flapping and pecking stiffly at currant bread with the nervous sobriety of scavengers. The ships rumble out to sea, the waves lap, the sun glistens in the cold . . . I wish, I wish . . . dreaming, wishing his life away.

Don't think of the future – that's too vague. The *immediate* future – God that's even vaguer, perhaps a little holiday somewhere, somewhere romantic, somewhere full of melancholy and late autumnal gold, mmm yes, leaves too.

The ferry docks and the gangway falls down. As he waits to board amongst the disembarking passengers he sees Irene, the comp girl, he used to work with. She mouths, 'How are you?' as she passes. And he mouths back, 'I'm fine. How are you?' And she's gone. And I think of the times spent in her company at that office – and Barbara, elegant and speaking French in the lunch hour – and how one can become attached to one's workmates, how you can come to love their company.

Friday. Wages day for those girls. Locked in the accounts department, laughing through the tea break and dreaming of things we'd never buy or be able to afford. And injustices, grudges held like sacred things. You moaned, you cursed but you stayed there all the same. You even begin to miss the people whom you disliked and those who disliked you.

He gets on board the ferry and it melts away from the landing stage where the pigeons peck and gorge and flap and cry.

A cast of unusual women work with me. Lindy – a girl who laughs hysterically in plainsong at the switchboard and who looks as though, at any minute, she'll be dragged away and given electric-shock therapy. June – who somehow gives the impression that she'd be happier at home, sitting in a corner, being fertile. The corrugated, duodenal face of Mrs M – talking occasionally in a such a high-pitched, highly-strung voice that at times it's almost ultrasonic – coughs and wheezes through the day.

We four sit in our room which has one window. Air like invisible treacle clings to the body making one suppurate inside one's suit. Tweed coloured sweat in the armpits and running into the pubic hair itchy and uncomfortable. All this tinged with the faint smell of dead mice which have eaten poison during the night and collapsed behind the stacked stationery. Through a door the small, greased head of the general manager with a side-kick called Cyril – a chubby, rampant kupie-doll who devours anyone he thinks might be a threat, who has a palaeolithic sense of humour. We are the members of the smallest subsidiary in a network of companies, housed in a single hot building.

Throughout the day, faces pass to and fro on the stairs without ever knowing you or your deepest hopes and ambitions. It has the feel of an iron curtain country bleak made bleaker still by the fact that one has lost the will to defy it, one's only wish is to surrender and say 'O.K. let's call it a day', and yet something – pride, vanity – makes you stick it out and think 'Kid the enemy, don't let the bastards grind you down.' Yet it's hard, some days. Bloody hard.

Here I sit in the canteen.

There they sit improving their homes with the devotion of missionaries. 'Woodstain, conti-board, hardboard, varnish, finish like glass, bloody made-up with them shelves.'

One sits there in this tedium feeling far, far away from it all. One cannot join in. One is numb, stiff from sheer boredom.

Read Dickens at lunchtime and tried to think of G.C.E.'s to be taken at night school. Couldn't summon up enough interest.

Feeling scared in the billiard room. Dust sheets over the cues.

Oh God, if only there was something, anything . . . worn out going home, want to cry sometimes too, can't explain . . . too cold in the mornings, too hot in the afternoons . . . Christ, getting on, getting old, feel hurt, sort of grey. Half-past-three, one and a half hours to go, petty cash won't balance, pounds out, don't care really, not my money, not my worry . . . still it's my job I suppose . . . it's what I'm paid for. Might buy a record on Friday . . . could go and see our Eileen, perhaps meet the lads for a drink. What a mess, what a bloody mess.

It's now that one sees all one's mistakes strung out like rosary beads. Once there was such a wealth of hope and opportunity, once there was a great feeling of freshness, once there was an age of gold. To have left so much behind! To have made so many miscalculations! Gone the rapport with favourite workmates. Gone the laughter over tea. Gone assurance on a grand scale and the eight hour day seeming like a sentence.

How to get through a day in one piece.

You try to be friendly but only succeed in looking ingratiating. Trying to be jolly amidst so much unpopularity. One feels utterly hated, completely overwhelmed.

Tea-time and alone again. Not being able to think of a single thing to say as the four men crouch together while one of them tells a joke about gonorrhoea. They all look intense, anticipating the punch line . . . stillness . . . then a roar of faces while on the periphery you sit there unable to laugh, not having heard the pay-off. Smile at them – if you don't they'll think you're a prude.

'Why don't you try and make friends, lad,' Mother will say, not knowing just how difficult it is to do so, not knowing that you are totally without the key to the puzzle.

Mum – oh mum – what's happened over the last twenty-seven years? What on earth has happened mum?

Once again car talk at the canteen table. Once again the *camaraderie* of the automobile. While the man with the long, cream fingernails talks, the others listen – a trio of heads bent forward, nodding and laughing at the joke of motoring.

'I've walked away from seven crashes,' he says.

At the end of the table Julie rolls an orange from one hand to the other. Julie who's got a degree, Julie who couldn't find a job when she graduated, Julie who studied philosophy at Cambridge; grinning occasionally through folds of boredom, watching the orange travel back and forth across the melamine.

The man who walked away from seven crashes is now well into his fourth jolly motoring story with those three heads nodding faster and faster, going pink, shaking as he shudders in mime down the M1. His hands cut the air, the fingernails, horrible in their length, become mesmeric as they sweep and fall, describing, moulding, singing, drooping in a great re-creation of his experiences – in many, many cars. At last, the hands crumple together, laconic, terse. Another peformance is over and the heads ease back smiling.

In the canteen the people become different, more strange. As they sit about in groups they create, by their very existence, a numbing fear of eating alone. Yet at the table with your colleagues you don't know any funny stories about mass-death on the motorways, can't think of any rejoinders to the many *double entendres*. You can only sit there watching their faces and hope for a smile or a friendly word, a gesture, a token of something, anything just so long as you are included.

Another meal to be got through. Another miserable day in a succession of miserable days.

As yesterday no one speaks.

Occasionally a box-camera voice comes over the intercom, 'Calling Mr Maxwell, Mr Maxwell, telephone call for Mr Maxwell'. Then silence.

Once again alone at lunchtime as the billiard balls drop into pockets and the wind beats, in squalls, against the rafters. A wasteland, a desert.

Ritchie, Jimmy, Frank, Alex, Les, Dennis – names you can't put faces to. Men at the snooker table swearing, laughing, as they chalk their cues, esoteric in waistcoats, thick Scottish accents bawling in clans.

'Wonderful fucking shot!'

'Oh fuck!'

'Fucking great stuff!'

As if these obscenities have the power to transform *them* into men, into a man's man, into one of the boys. It takes on the hysteria of ritual, shouting, shouting, with only themselves to hear. Daren't be on the fringes, might think you're a freak, a snob, an idiot, or worst of all – a poof. Shouting, shouting, like the boys in the park then touching and moving about one another with an easy, a revolting familiarity, cursing and occasionally grabbing a crutch.

And that heavy grin, like at school, in the changing room next to the gym, where you weren't allowed to wear anything under your shorts and someone would always try to pull them down, down to their level, down to the ultimate humiliation, naked and absurd below the clothes hooks.

One needs something to restore the soul.

Someone throws a billiard ball in my direction, it doesn't

hit me but plops down onto the floor, rolls and stops at my feet. I stop eating and look down at it. Their laughter stops. All eyes on me. Should I look at them? Should I pick it up? Should I go on eating? Time passes and I don't move.

'It nearly hit him,' someone says and roars of laughter break out. And the game continues.

Once again jobs in the offing. Hope for a brighter future. An idea was forming. Should he leave? After such a long time in the same firm *could* he leave?

They all worked silently in the small room. Occasionally the telephone would ring, someone might call along the corridor outside or a window might rattle as the drizzle and wind shook the glass.

'Shall I close the window?'

'Mm?'

'Shall I close the window?' His words seem heavy in the chest. Silence. Standing up in the small room with the noise of pens.

'Yes' drops from her lips, without looking up.

Outside, grey rain which has fallen all day. Cold feet damp inside shoes. Snuggling close to the radiator. The window closed, the air is still, and in silence we carry on working.

And yet. And yet his heart, his very soul knew that this *must* change, that he must get away from this entrapment. Where now? When now? Cosy and warm. And yet. Keep going! Jobs in the offing. Ideas forming. And their laughter. And their small jokes. Rain drizzling all day. The misery of cold . . .

And yet the day he leaves he will remember only the nice things, the camaraderie, the laughs, everything else will be soothed away until no clouds remain and the future which, in abstract, seemed so bright will become clear, sharp, and will not then seem such a release from stagnation. Just bleak in its clarity and nothing or no one able to help.

Then after many years spent in this office 'among friends' it was only logical that he should discover how little he had in common with these people, how alien he felt among them. These were the days which were long and desolate – an ache. He wished for familiarity and contentment. To have to go through this for the rest of one's life!

'Terrible! Terrible!' kept going through his head; made more terrible by the fact that he knew the certainty of suffering, its precision. Awful, absolute knowledge – *awful*! Crushing, this ability to be crushed. Yet to know there was no way out. To know that this was the way it would always be. No end. But the pattern will go back, avalanching down in detail after detail.

Typists' sons studying in the States, travelling across Europe, degrees from U.C.L.A. and good jobs waiting, wearisome this monumental display of parental chauvinism. How can she think of her sons like that? As if they were the answer to an academician's prayer. Oh will her talking never stop? It's like being stood against a wall and pummelled with grammar. One is insensible from it.

On and on she goes, her voice a battering ram, nouns, pronouns, adverbs, adjectives come tumbling out.

At last. She goes back to her own office leaving mine strewn with verbs. I feel dismantled, broken. My head is still throbbing from her voice, still feeling, still hearing her sentences bounce on and off my head in hammer blows – three beats to the bar in high dynamics as if she'd been conducting the London Symphony Orchestra.

Sitting here surrounded by commerce, by the women in green holding cups of tea, who are shorthand-typists, who tell each other that their children have been picked for school pantomimes. Outside it's dark even though, it's only ten am.

He sat with his filled teacup, encased in his own personality, desperately wanting to strike up a conversation with someone. He wanted so much to be told about sherry trifle, of dinner dances and whispered confidences that make you feel part of the whole. But no. Aloneness splashing about you.

'I've got to make a break,' he thought. 'I've got to get out of my rut.'

And London came to mind.

And the comp-girl – always so friendly – now so cool, looking through me, talking across me as if I'm not here. So now I take a back seat. Cold-shouldered in late December, so very near Christmas.

Sitting here with my face swollen, my eyes sore as if I'd been crying all night. It's hard being snubbed. It's hard being cut out of someone's shallow affections. No more exchanges and friendly pats on the arm – just simply outlawed with the knowledge that next time it will be *even harder* to recover. Please be friendly.

Tell me about your Saturday night out at the club. And have I seen the group which was on? And what do I think of little girls knocked down in tragic headlines? And please – oh please – don't shut me away from the smiles.

When finally she does speak it is to wound.

'Going out this weekend?'

'No. I don't think so.'

'Why not?'

'Oh I don't know. Just can't seem to be bothered.'

'You should get out more. You're getting into a rut. You're getting old.'

It's strange how a simple phrase can crush and make you feel deeply hurt. You're opened, wounded. And the phrase hangs in the mind, in the air, and you are sure everyone is aware of your capacity to be vulnerable and yes, to be weak. You keep the eyes down, the shoulders bent, and you want to cry, slash out against the injustice of the remark and she who made it.

You just sit there over your tea trying not to let it hurt anymore, trying to soothe it away – the way mothers and bogeymen do. And when you have to speak your words hang in the mouth, sound clavicular in the warm office air and reveal what you're *really* feeling.

The weekend upon us. Days to rest, presents to be wrapped, the Holy Land and carols sung at the door as you finish dinner on blue pottery dishes with gypsy glazing. Monday to be dreaded. Must paint the bathroom ceiling. Stain the floor and varnish it. Purple and white. Pain and innocence. Don't let Monday come. I'm just not up to it. But that word repeats itself over and over again with a terrible precision. Old. *Old*.

Why should it seem so awful? To lose the hair, to lose the *secret*, to lose the threads of youth is so insidious, so silent, so gradual. Your language becomes fixed, staid and you simply lose the capacity for excitement, you simply lose the will to be passionate.

This group of men, this band of women to whom I thought I would never belong, bought me pens, signed a card, gave me money in an envelope marked *Your fare home*, then shook my hand and wished me well. And as I left the telephonist threw her arms around me and wished me 'all the best'. Her gesture, more eloquent than kisses, touched me. Then standing on the landing stage and waiting to cross the river for the last time. No more waiting for the ferry boats ploughing to and fro across the Mersey. No more that seven minute walk from the bus terminal to the office – sweating in summer, cursing in winter. No more creaking of the pier in wet weather. No more jokes shared in the middle of the stairs or laughter through a door. Just a vision, a picture of a girl in red standing there throwing her arms around me. She'll be pretty and red and twenty-three forever. She'll stay there fixed and infinitely touching as I carry my presents – my treasures – home with me on a blustery day at the end of August.

The Liverpool Pullman.

The Liverpool Pullman.

Ladies in cream dresses, holding matching cream handbags, look towards their daughters who glower in red coats and stiff, permed hair – shoving them towards their seats.

'Granny's dead.'

Gran. Inhaling snuff, surrounded by mahogany, sitting in her chair, smelling of newly washed cushion covers, stale bread and stout.

'Go and get me a Jew's loaf,' she'd say – meaning an oven-bottom, 'and I'll give you a sugar butty.' Which always sent me running down her blue, half-distempered hall wondering how she could have been my dad's mother since he'd died before she had.

The Liverpool Pullman.

The Liverpool Pullman.

I can only recall my father vaguely – full of brooding silences, and long ferocious rages and small, tender, rare kindnesses. And a smile at Christmas.

Mother is not at all vague. She is supremely concrete and so much harder to define. Always there, full of love, brimming with pride at her children's small successes, her infinite patience with teething babies, dust and sheer hard graft to keep us clean. Her marvellous healing hands, her wonderful skin, her immortality and her youth.

Then we all left her – dear God we left her alone to wander around that big, old house with only the radio for company and her lonely memories, her silent tears and her old, half-longing for her children gone away – her *cherished* boys and girls. Every room is full of echoes, the house full of voices – and all of them *young*, even her own.

The clutter of teenage girls' make-up in that battered triangle of mirror. The blouses, the skirts, the shoes, the *Evening in Paris* scent in tiny, purple bottles . . . and out through the door leaving the scented debris on the table and the smell of clothes pressed with a flat iron. Pancake thumb prints on the sideboard, a tortoise shell comb. 'Take care of yourselves,' always called but only half-listened to. 'But they're good girls and the lads are no trouble,' as they saunter downstairs, Brylcreamed (marge if there wasn't any), cuffs at least an inch showing, big cufflinks and a Windsor knot in your tie – just like Frank Sinatra.

'Enjoy yourselves,' as their slip-ons clatter to the street.

'Immaclulate,' she thinks. 'Our John's always immaculate,' and Kevin the good-looker. Tony courting gentle Rose from far Saxony Road. Even I desert her now – to play Lancelot with Leonard Culf, with poles, charging at each other from either end of the street, imitating purring horses.

But she always has something to do, someone to clear up after. Yet at the back of her commonsense, innocent mind, is the aching, the falling dread of when her girls begin to leave her and her boys get someone pregnant, and after the grand procession of marriages – a cold and empty house. And slowly she will age, slowly her immense energy will wither and she will become as frail and fragile as stardust. Then the silence will consume her, and she will become a memory, a part of history.

The Liverpool Pullman.

The Liverpool Pullman.

Mum's walking with me through the station, limping as she carries one of my bags.

'Mum why don't you go to the doctor's?'

'Oh I'll be alright. Just getting old. Decripit.' And she smiles and limps and gives me another pound so that I won't be short.

The Liverpool Pullman.

The Liverpool Pullman.

She should see about that leg. None of us is getting any younger. And her white hair. And her luminous, sad eyes. Don't leave lad. Don't go.

Mum. Mum.

The Liverpool Pullman.

The Liverpool Pullman.

Standing on the echoing platform, with the luggage cluttering the feet, smiling occasionally but saying nothing.

'Now look after yourself, son.'

'Yes mum.'

'Make sure you get proper food.'

'Yes Mum, I will.'

There was so much to say, there were so many things they should say to each other, but didn't, or rather they only filled in the silences which hung above the noise of the station and the heartbreak.

You'll never know just how much I love you. You'll never know just how much I care.

Don't let me go mam! Never let me go! Love me, love me, love me say you do!

But just a whistle and a parting hug. When she walked away holding her platform ticket my heart went with her.

An adventure was beginning. A journey anticipated for weeks with mingled joy and apprehension. He had come to London to search for gold, to seek his fortune. He had saved hard. Every penny he'd taken with him he'd *earned*. And now he was here – at Metropolis. An adventure had begun. And now he was here in this red hotel room which had a shower and two beds and long green curtains – and a *phone*! And now he was here sitting on the bed eating the sandwiches he'd brought with him. Tea things on the opposite bed. Traffic outside skirting Hyde Park. He felt utterly fragile. Everything was so bright, so uncannily oppressive. Yet this was the heart of *everything* – like Paris in the '90's.

Reception rings through. 'Sorry to disturb you sir, but would you like a T.V. in your room?'

'Yes please.' Trying not to sound too bucolic, yet friendly, if a little off-hand.

'Very well, sir, I'll have one sent up straight away.'
'Thank you.'
'Thank you.'

And the white phone pings down. Extension 110. If I want I can ring, I can speak to anyone I like. But I don't know anyone here. So I don't ring.

Shuddering in clashing, windy tubes far below the city, Lancaster Gate, Marble Arch, Bond Street, Oxford Circus, Tottenham Court Road. CHANGE. And never a smile. Leicester Square, Charing Cross, Waterloo, Kennington, Oval, Stockwell, Clapham. Silence on the Northern Line all the way from Tooting Bec. CHANGE. Escalators. Lights. Southbound for Morden and the mysteries of Colliers Wood and South Wimbledon. CHANGE. At Holborn or Warren Street or Barons Court or Moorgate, and . . . Oh panic . . . and . . . Oh heartbreak, and . . . Christ oh Christ these endless, monstrous tubes. First train to Edgeware, second train to High Holborn. Cockfosters and Brixton, Hounslow Central and Hounslow West. CHANGE. And terror in the eyes and foreign, non-commital Americans and bland, impassive Japanese and gentle bewildered Asians preceding their wives or chattering in nervous groups or silent and alone, overwhelmed by all this dazzling barbarity. Chalk Farm. Belsize Park. CHANGE. Bronzed Italians bored with their own good looks, pinched Englishmen who visit Golders Green on official business, suave, marble women who work in clinics and incredible young men, sullen and phallic.

And the play of the meagre light. The emptiness of the soul. Gloucester Road. Knightsbridge. Hyde Park Corner. This monstrous, evil city. This corrosive terror.

In Babylon.

Soon the money begins to run out. Soon I move to cheaper and cheaper hotels. Soon I get an office job. Soon I move into digs miles from where I work. Soon I start hanging around bars, loitering over drinks and long, lingering looks from older men. Soon I begin to answer advertisements of a very *special* sort:–

> 'Young bi-sexual leatherguy (24)
> would like suggestions on how
> to keep warm during long, winter
> evenings. Box BP/129'
> 'Bearded guy, bodybuilder (28)
> into leather and skin-tight jeans.
> Seeks similar. No camps. Box BP/132'
> 'Biker – good physique – (32) seeks
> mates anywhere with black leather
> and bikes. Box BP/160'
> 'Handsome London biker – interests
> bodybuilding/leather/rubber S & M
> wants friends anywhere. Box BP/200'

Soon I build up a vast number of contacts whom I never see or meet, people who pour out their very souls on paper, people who know my blackest secrets and my most dreaded hopes. Occasionally a subscriber actually gives a telephone number but these people are the loneliest, the most tormented. Torrents of abuse, hushed and whispered, falling into the receiver ending in solitary masturbation.

One never rings if a phone number is given. Looking at the letters both sent and received. So many letters sent to so many men. Letters with their formal obscenities and their gloating exclamation marks.

What would they say at home if they knew I did this sort of thing?

And then I met St John.

On a high, bright day.

Invited to Emma's party and I am the second to arrive. Met St John – horrible little man with psoriasis – who talks only of money and Gilbert and Sullivan. Spoilt everything. Had tea with him and this lady who worked for the BBC during the war (the second one), who re-uses used envelopes. Frightful house – like something out of Edgar Allan Poe. Dark, gothic, hideous in the extreme and full of paper and moquette. They sang Victorian duets together at a saloon-type piano with candleholders.

Dust rising from this ancient moquette, this seventy-year-old furniture. Emma finishes singing and the dwarf smiles at me, then devours three buttered scones. We lift our cups in unison, then Emma excuses herself and rises eloquently into the blue light as if she were married to a don, in a unversity study with crossed oars above a stuffed trout in a glass case and leather-bound editions of *Paradise Lost* and Milton. And Ezra Pound wainscoted. She ripples through the rippling, quivering light and heads for the crypt while the dwarf scratches his inflamed belly skin, fingers his monocle and then my crutch while tossing back his head – he has no neck – and talks about Eton, money, managership, money, head chefs cooking with dirty untensils, money, *Capa Magna*, journalism and money and all the time rubbing me and saying, 'You *are* a big boy' as part of me responds, wetly, rigidly inside the underpants. Emma comes – in fact we both do. She picks her way through shafts of sunlight, resumes her seat, shaking inside her woollen cardigan, recalling the North African campaign, Montgomery, desert rats, Sidi Burani, defeating Rommel, singing to the troops, broadcasting on the long wave, The Few, victory in Europe and smiling Royalty on a balcony before Labour got in and formed a government on a landslide.

People begin to arrive – tinkling at the door then hovering over the table laden with eatables and calling to one another before smirking in my direction as Emma introduces them to me, me to them, in her best, ethereal, Virginia Woolf voice.

Tiny cakes and huge mouths, old trying to be young,

creatures in blue over china cups filled with scented tea, crumbs at the edges of mouths, home-made jam on the fingertips.

'Yum-Yum,' for the Arab boys who gave our host a pestle with a hole in it. Charles drawling in a well-heeled voice. Elspeth, in jodhpurs, gloomy during trifle. Colin, Delia, Antony, Richard . . . grinning metaphysically and smoking cigarillos as the Sunday bells peal over mock half timber and china teacups and the legends of Miriam. The owners of England.

'I went youth hostelling. There were lots of Austrian boys hanging around like extras from Visconti's *The Damned*.'

People with blistering intellects, who know Mervyn Peake's daughter and whose voices gently caress and bewilder with their perception, their judgements, their vivid analyses. You hope for inspiration, long to have gone to Cambridge, to have had your mind forged, to have had your confidences armed with the weaponry of knowledge.

'Our generation was a generation of actors and directors . . .'

'I think one has to look at one's situation at a slight angle to the Universe . . .'

'Decision making? One makes a decision but the reality of that decision and its consequences are, I find, too frightening to contemplate . . .'

'Oh God . . . I feel like Lytton Strachey!'

Faces. What faces! That blue creature, carrying a small, blue pedigree dachshund, stares about him with a furious sort of effeminacy, camp as a row of tents and twice as gloomy. He stands there not speaking until spoken to, then he breaks into malevolent smiles and the jokes come thick and fast and are violently misogynist.

His eyes dart about, he fears getting older, getting bald, counting the seconds to the next affair, trying to make youth stay longer than it's able to. Stubborn in his refusal to age, he looks even older – especially in profile.

Small, exquisite sandwiches travel in limpid hands from the shade into the light and are popped delicately into chattering mouths . . .

'She cuts the Hovis so *beautifully* thin!'

Sniggering from a group hidden in the gloom. A shadowy voice . . .

'Her mother – that's the one with the voice like a dull patch of concrete.' Furious sniggering.

'Titian? With hair that colour he should be standing near a zebra crossing . . . '

That calling dwarf in one of the groups looks in my direction.

'Come along Cinders.'

Never mind me I'll blend with the wallpaper. But I go over and join them all the same. A balletomane who once saw a great performance of *La Fille Mal Gardée* purses his lips, then flutters in memory and touches you whenever he can. To the left more campery.

'. . . but the old have no morals.'

'What about the young?'

'Oh them! They're even worse. They think that morals come like free gifts, with cornflakes. They are victims of their own chic. They don't know the difference between a moral and a fashion and for them they've both become pretty much the same thing.'

Then in comes a young man and we all turn, roar in silence at this incredible 'thing'. *Perfect*. Surrounded by the lazy sexuality of soft, pink skin sliding under tight-fitting clothes. Rippling desirability. Sexuality – like a dry fire – curls and crackles between the legs, between the trembling, quivering thighs.

He is introduced as Nicholas. His rump rises and falls as he changes position, pouts as he stands running his right hand through his hair, his left hand holding his lighter, his

Gauloises palmed with the two fingers holding a cigarette.

I cannot take my eyes from this smoking, transparent creature standing in the light, smiling, talking. A God in Maida Vale. In a sucking, thrusting, groaning, clawing, clutching, stretching, stinking, falling, writhing, rising, breathy orgy with him, my imagination shocks even me.

He turns, half turns. He smiles, half smiles. Then blazes towards me. I look down into my tea not knowing how I'll cope.

'Oh Nicky!' calls the blue voice and Nicholas turns back to dachshund and friend surrounded now by a select circle of nodding dentures. A set of teeth says something I don't quite catch and the blue man turns to Nicholas with a look which drips smiling, vindictive ownership. With his free hand he stops stroking the dog and grabs Nicholas's hair and slowly drags the head back. Nicholas's smiling, upturned face enjoying his humiliation as we all stop talking and look at him.

'She's mine and no rent!'

For a moment no one breathes. Nicholas's head is pulled right back. The blue hand tightens its grip on his hair. Nicholas is radiant - even more beautiful at this, the moment of his ultimate disgrace. The hand releases the head and Nicholas grins around the room – tamed and untameable. Then Emma politely passes around the polite sandwiches. Savages cascade into, then out of rooms, into then out of the mind, your life, with never a murmur, or nod, or touch, or smile. They have a sub-language only they can understand. Through striped silk and cheesecloth you can see their wafer-thin, tremulous personalities quivering over the paté.

'Oh Henrietta!'

'It's Sally. *Sally* ' Slurred and indifferent.

'Did you go to Bristol with Tina?.

' . . . Oh I know! . . . '

'Just finished a film . . . '

' . . . friends of friends . . . '
'BBC . . . '
' . . . too much Mateus!'

Picking your way through expensive looking wine bottles – the only friendly things here. It's the sort of party which makes you feel that you should drink nothing stronger than *Vimto*. Strange, strange people.

Out into the long garden crammed with people. In a sunken area two American 'boys' make rich hamburgers – all camp and onions.

'Who wants a hamboiyger?'
'Come and get it!'
'No mustard.'
'You gotta have mustard.'
'No I . . . '
'Taste it.'
'No really I . . . '
'Taste it! It is not hot! *It is not your English shit!*'
'Alright mustard then'

This is the most subtle kind of jungle.
This is what survival has come to mean.

'Streatham
London. 10th February.

Dear Robert (or do you prefer Robbie?),

It was delightful to have met you at Emma's and I hope you will forgive me for writing.

Although we chatted only briefly we seem to have similar interests. I am a journalist and T.V. Director. I also work as a music and theatre critic and I play the organ. (Oddly enough I played at Arundel R.C. Cathedral this afternoon. It was built by the present Duke of Norfolk's father.)

I'm answering my instincts to write to you – from a friend's flat, in fact. He's the manager of several cinemas in the West End.

What kind of job do you have. If you are not in journalism or the theatre, do you want to be? Perhaps I could help in some way. Although I'm not much older than you I seem to have made a vast number of contacts. I seem to have interviewed everyone from Dame Nellie Melba to the Beatles!

Would you like to come over to Streatham for the weekend? Do let me know if you can. Why not ring me – say Monday night after 10.00 pm, reversing the charges.

    Regards,
      St John.'

I felt touched by his letter but something, somewhere very remote in me, was afraid. A dull caution stirred and a curious, repelled feeling turned my very bowels. Walking to the phone booth I knew that what I was doing was a mistake. Why did I speak to him? Why did I smile politely? Why did I let him touch me? Why did I let him wring my address from me? *Dwarf*. But it gets lonely on your own, with the hand in the darkness of a room, it gets so anonymous travelling through the lights and the rain at Marble Arch and perhaps he's not really too bad and perhaps he's genuine – underneath.

Dwarf.

Putting the money in, saying 'hello', I knew was wrong and that I should heed my instinct to shrink. *Dwarf*. But before I know it I'm trapped into meeting him at the weekend.

                        'Streatham
                         London.
                 1.30 am. 15th Feb.
Dear Robert,
Splendid hearing from you on the 'phone and I'm looking

forward to Friday *very* much. I'll pick you up outside the Houses of Parliament at 5.15 pm.
>Looking forward to seeing you,
>Sincerely,
>St. John.'

Driving through outer London towards Brighton and the bleak Sussex Downs. St John, crouched and squinting behind the wheel, drowns me with words . . . 'Eton, studied under Thalban-Ball, played at Cambridge, bank account at Coutts', That's Roedean, we'll lunch tomorrow at Fortnum's, cherry jam and tea, silk shirts from Jermyn Street, only just moved into Streatham (tedius part of town but convenient for my journalism, for my work), Lord Coulson, dined last week at Windsor Forest . . .' and a veiled remark, accidentally made, about forged cheques, an Old Bailey Trial and an acquittal for lack of evidence, and nagging doubts and little tantalizing fears as Lewes then Brighton hang on the horizon, with the grey sea beyond.

We managed to find a parking space in a small, white street in Brighton.

'I'm going to sign-on,' he says as he gets out of the car. Why sign-on in Brighton when he lives in London? In the dashboard a window envelope. I pick it up. It is from Coutts – a letter and bank statement. £760 overdrawn and the manager demanding that St John surrender his cheque book and prim chidings for previous letters not answered.

From nowhere St John appears and I hastily push the letter, the bank statement, the envelope back into the dashboard.

'Any sign of a job yet?' but thinking about his first letter which gave me the impression he was already working.

'No,' he says as he struggles into the drivers seat and puts his money into his wallet, 'but I've got several ideas.'

'Money must be a bit tight then.' My voice shaking as I clumsily try to probe.

'A little. I have a bit of an overdraft.'
'Oh. How much?' Shaking, shaking.
'Oh . . . about £46 but Coutts' are very good.'

As we drive away he notices the letter, the statement from the bank, the open, white window envelope crushed in the dashboard and in silence we drive to Eastbourne.

> 'Streatham.
> February 21st.

Darling Robert,

I hope sincerely that you will forgive the fact that I'm typing this; the fact is that there is so very much I want to say.

As I said I'm awfully glad that I spent so much time talking to you and hearing about your life *before* we met. I suppose at one point I must have thought you to be rather mixed up. I know I did. But also I know that there were reasons and that I might be able to help you achieve some kind of confidence. It was only after we talked that I understood so much and loved (yes loved) you all the more for it.

Please don't think I'm saying this simply to get you to come to live with me though, believe me, I want that more than ever. As I said over the weekend I'm *convinced* that such meetings happen to two people once in their lifetimes and that such meetings must be acted upon, so to speak.

You said think about it. You said that because you thought I was simply being nice to (and here I use your word) a 'yokel'. I meant (and mean) all I said. My summation now is that I met a charming person on Friday with whom I spent a perfect weekend. Because, in our rather strange world things happen fairly quickly, I told you exactly what I felt.

Don't be frightened. Just as I never left you all weekend I know that our relationship would be based on companionship, and believe me, I found you a wonderful companion. I'm not desperate. It's only because I realise that I have met someone so wonderful that I simply want to spend my life with you. That's not wrong. We both agree there. You want assurance. You may want assurances for 25 years. I am quite prepared to give them. I want you and I now realise in the cold, harsh reality of 1.00 am that I need you and that I was not extravagant in my claims or statements. I'm at my wits end as I don't know how to convince you and don't want to lose you. I hope this feeling is mutual. Do let me know. *Please*.

So far as coming over this forthcoming weekend is concerned. Why not let me pick you up in the car? Don't be proud. My feelings for you are such that I don't want to be parted from you.

Do give me a chance to prove what I want to do. Do please believe me. Do make me happy by coming this weekend.

Believe me when I say that I have never written at such length to anyone. What an effect you've had on me!
> With all my love,
> Sincerely,
> St John.'

At night he won't undress with the lights on and even in the dark he is physically repellent. I try not to think about it. I lie with my eyes closed as he gets into bed, a flesh mountain. I mustn't think these things! He'd be so *hurt*. Yet it shows. You cannot conceal it, you cannot make love reluctantly. I DON'T TRUST HIM! Now and again he makes me freeze with horror. 'I want to give it to you.' To be *entered* and by *him*! Oh Christ no! NO! So it's put off for a while but I know that one night he will turn to threats, that one night he will start to spin his fantastic web of words about me, that one night excuses will not be enough, that one night it will happen and that it will be ugly. 'I want to give it to you, I want to give it to you.'

'Streatham
Sunday 9.45pm.

My Darling,

When I left you I drove back to the house thinking of you every minute, thinking of the way you looked during the weekend.

I know this week is going to be rather terrible for you. It's going to be awful for me too. I always think waiting is dreadful, especially when it's a matter of waiting for the one you love. I looked forward to the first weekend but I shall look forward even more to this one. I've got to the point of thinking (quite sincerely) that without you there is nothing. You may say it's rather drastic, but that's the way I feel and it's silly to disguise one's feelings. One can go through life for years without telling people how one really feels and, of course, it's important to grasp one's happiness when one can.

I know that all the time you are going to be telling yourself that on the one hand it will be wonderful, and on the other, dare you do it. Well, we both know that neither is going to let the other down, and that the weekends we have already spent together, which we have both enjoyed tremendously, are only brief tastes of how wonderful the future will be providing that we both stick together.

So far as the financial aspect is concerned. Don't worry. You don't eat enough to keep a bird alive. If you give me £15 or £20 a week for your board etc. that will be more than adequate. So don't worry.

I know you said that you did not really want me to ring etc but it would be wonderful if you could ring me sometimes during the week and, of course, reverse the charges.

And if you could write. I'm sure you can find a few minutes. I'll ring you sometime on Friday to find out the time of your arrival.

Darling believe me please when I say that you are and will be taking a big step but that you won't regret it and my

word, once given, is just as binding as yours. Do believe me.
>   All my love,
>   St John.'

Standing naked and gross, in front of the bed, his small cough – hanging in the air – drips with fire.

'Lick it clean.' He demands. Febrile and alarming. Even his penis is replusive. The gas fire sings. I close my eyes. Dear God, dear God. And my unwilling mouth receives him.

> 'Streatham
> 4.30pm Weds.

My Darling,

I decided not to go over to Christchurch. As I have no intention of working there, the journey seemed pointless.

Marvellous to hear you again last night and wonderful, so wonderful that you are coming over on Friday. I'll ring the office about 3.00 pm so I'll know what time to expect you.
>   Much, much love,
>   St John.'

Shopping at Harrods. St John pointing out the couples who are gay. Hovering tentatively with a wire basket in the food hall. 'Buy something for God's sake!' he says sotto voce and irritated, 'You look like an advert for arthritis-sufferers being brave.'

> 'Streatham.
> Tues. evening
> 11.00 pm.

Darling R.

I've just spent an hour being nice to Richard. Now now, I don't mean that kind of niceness. I asked him in for a drink and he's left to sweep the floor. (My paying guests do their own floors!)

Rather pleasant fellow from Poole came this afternoon and said he wanted to take the large room on the ground floor. He gave me a cheque as a deposit. All rather pleasant.

Visited some old friends of mine yesterday. Barry and Iain. We are to dine with them within the next fortnight.

I dare say that your week is pretty awful at the moment but I know that you have tremendous resolve and that is stronger. Anyway enough of that – I'm looking forward to Saturday.

By the time you read this I should have rung you again to learn your news. Words are not coming this evening.
   All my love,
    St John.'

At the dinner table, sitting below their clever words about music and the changing face of England and the Yorkshire ridings.

'I think that the American orchestras are rather hysterical in their interpretations of Mahler.' St John wolfing food in forkfuls.

'Yes, perhaps,' Richard, smart in black and white, 'but I like their *schmaltz*. They do it far better than we do.'

Then their conversation drops back into an RAC relief map. Leeds, Hull, Wolverhampton, Bradford, Liverpool, London, Birmingham, Brighton, Dymchurch – and Doctor Synn sliding through apple orchards.

(In the bedroom St John furious with me. 'There are limits to passivity for God's sake!')

'I prefer, I think, the earlier of the Bruckner cycle. One and two though not three.'

'I disagree. I like the later symphonies from seven onwards. The earlier ones seems to me to be hammering out a style. Bruckner seems to be trying to de-Wagnerize himself whereas seven to nine are mystical, looking towards a more ethereal world. He's secure in his religion in an almost childlike way – not infantile – but in the same sense as *Das Himmlische Leben.*'

(St John whispering in the dark. 'I want to give it to you. I want to shove it up so far it'll come out of your mouth.' Smothering me. Stop it. *Stop it*! 'You're not going to let me do it are you? You bastard you're not going to let me do it!'

And a hardness in his voice as he touches a nerve, an innermost fear. 'If you don't let me I'll tell your mother just what she's got for a son. I'll make sure you'll never be able to go home again. I'll let them *all* know and you won't be able to go near your little nephews ever again. I'll see to that, Angel.' Cold with fear.

'Turn over!'

No. No.

'Turn over. I'm going to fuck you!'

The rest is pain, the rest is ultimate humiliation. And after the panting of his thrusting, grotesque body – the silence drenched in sin. Then he picks up the phone, smiling.

'Shall I? Shall I phone Mummy and tell her, Angel?'

No, please. PLEASE. The irregular verb 'to beg'.

'There, angelpiecrust, there.'

And he replaces the receiver.)

'Yes, I think I would agree with you.'

Their laughter, their Turkish cigarettes, their expensive after shave bought at Harrods with worthless cheques – these are the men who will inherit the earth.

I want to go home.

How do you get to know these people? How do you get close? What are the combinations which will unlock these mysteries?

March is over. April has begun. No more analysis, no more nostalgia for things that were or might have been, the introductions are finished. Days have passed filled with hours of licence, sex-drenched with the sperm falling down, shouting into the bedclothes. So much writhing. So much animalism. And no more shame. Strange how one misses that.

In the night when it begins all over again, with their hands rising and falling, the great dark, with the whispered threats underneath the sheets, then a dark greater than the night will come down and once again you will be as lonely as before, as far away from any home as you have already been. Love. Love? When the lights dim and only the hands talk then I must believe it's true.

Birds in the trees, jets flying low into Gatwick or Heathrow. Silence in every room but most of all in yours. But no tears to shed, not even feelings to be hurt. Over, over, over, will be all that you'll think of as you sit there on the bed, and he downstairs listening to Gilbert and Sullivan and feeling wronged. And always the long, lost feeling of things that might have been, that words might have been spoken or left unsaid, that somehow you could have found happiness and love and contentment between the mauve sheets. Hopes gone, with no more to sustain you. No more 'love' to be given or received. Alone again. But what do I say to those who have been kind and wished me Godspeed?

What do I say when I try to explain so much wreckage? How do I get away from him so that he won't tell my mother?

I waited for my moment, for the right opportunity to slip away. Eventually it came. He was driving over to Oxford and as soon as the hired car was out of sight I packed and left.

Frantic on the train with coffee in a paper cup. Mum, mum. How do I tell you? What do I say?

And easily lies spring to mind as they always do. The truth

seems large and terrible while the lies look small and cosy as they multiply like rabbits. One feels so unclean amidst it all, so lost in vice it's hard to remember what it was like to have been in grace, so difficult after so long. No longer able to distinguish between truth and untruth, so long the fall from grace, so long to have been without absolution. Such hypocrisy – talking like Jesus and behaving like Judas.

But what if he writes? Or telephones? Or comes to the house in grey flannel?

So much to deny. So much to have to wade through. So much truth to have to face. I can only see lies stretching away, out into the distance like a roll of black cloth, endless, interminable, and all the while the same old ache. Will you never learn? Never?

But – once home – the post brings fresh terror.

'Faversham,
Kent.
17th April.

Dear Robert,

I have been meaning to write to you for some time on the subject of St John and when I heard that you had decided to leave him and return home I decided I would do so. I have been effectively fooled by St John for a long time – though I have had serious misgivings almost from the first time I met him. I suppose an instinctive mistrust.

Perhaps I should explain that I recently looked after a house near Canterbury which St John arranged to mind for a woman who had gone to Australia. I thought that she was a friend of his but now suspect that St John had some financial arrangement with her. Anyway I was there for six weeks, on my own much of the time, though St John came down at weekends and for longer spells when he appeared to have left his job.

Well the top and bottom of it is that the doubts I'd

entertained over a long period were confirmed in all kinds of ways. The way in which St John manipulates people in the most cynical way became apparent; how he exploits people, both emotionally and financially and how every move he makes is calculated and based not on feeling but out of self-interest and gratification.

I've always been uneasy about him, but was unable to see through the fantastic web of words he spins around people, disguising his real motives. Seeing him at close quarters for a period of weeks certainly opened my eyes. While it was an unpleasant experience in many ways it was also a useful one.

All kinds of things occur to me. While I was at this house I saw how he lied quite outrageously to people he met – gratuitous lies as well as those to gain something. In fact I've come to the conclusion that he is a pathological liar and his fantasies and lies are so much part of him that he actually believes some of it! I saw how he obtained credit by lying and without any intentions of paying bills, etc. For example, I was completely taken aback when, after leaving a shop where he had used all his charm and gifts of anecdote on an old man and his son and obtained goods to the value of about £40, he told me that he had no intention of paying. Indeed I doubt his ability to do so! I later rang the shop and put them wise.

The thing was that I was becoming an unwitting third party to his deceptions and I suppose that my association with him cast doubts on my integrity. All kinds of things of this sort occurred. Some more serious. I have been a fool to have been taken in by him for so long. I'm only sorry that I ever met him at all.

I honestly think him capable of any kind of unpleasantness. He even told Emma that there had been a liaison between him and I – which is absolute rubbish! I suppose he may have told you something similiar.

As you see I am now living back in Kent with a chap of whom I'm very fond. He took an instant dislike to St John and he and I have been doing a little checking.

This morning we had a letter from the Registrar of Eton College to the effect that they'd never heard of St John there and would like to know if he continues to claim to be an old Etonian. His claims to aristocratic connections are equally unfounded from what we can gather. I'm sure the name he uses is an alias.

Now the Eton bit is so central and basic to St John's assumed persona and has become so much part of his personal fantasies that now he actually believes it himself.

He is also again in touch with 'Lord Coulson' and 'Keith Cavendish' both recently out of gaol for fraud in which, if you don't already know, St John too was implicated.

Patrick, the friend I mentioned, is now following up these leads. Among other things that came to light is that my name has been used as an alias by Keith Cavendish – he could only have got it from St John – he used my name apparently while visiting Maidstone Gaol. Not a pleasant thought.

Since I now recognise that he never cultivates anybody for their own sake, on a basis of friendship, I've begun to wonder what his motives are. I think him capable of almost anything. He has a monstrous ego and is completely ruthless.

I felt I ought to write to you and tell you all this, especially as you were wise enough to go home to Liverpool.

Anway we're both well shot of him. I hope this letter confirms your views.

I'm sorry that we met so briefly and under such circumstances. I hope things have worked out well for you when you got home and that you're happier now – I'm sure you are. Don't feel obliged to answer this though I'd be interested to hear from you. If ever you're in this part of the world look us up.

        Yours sincerely,
          Richard.'

'Streatham
London.
19 April.

My Dear Robbie,

Emma and all the others who met you were very sorry to hear that you had returned to Liverpool. Emma especially. She felt that London could have made you.

I hope that you reached home safely. As I said earlier you are, and always will be, most welcome here. Do write and let me know how you are.

I'm working very hard.
      Much Love,
           St John.'

Gradually the letters cease.

'Streatham
London.
29th April.

Dear Robbie,

I'm awfully sorry not to have heard from you since your return home. I've missed you terribly but don't expect you to believe that.

Now that you're back in Liverpool and (I hope) settling down I do wish you'd write a brief note to say that you are alright. Surely there is no need for us to be so very far apart when we were once so very close.
      Love,
           St. John.'

Gradually the fear contracts.

>   'Streatham
>   London.
>   5th May.
>
> Dear Robbie,
>
> You left some casual clothes in the wardrobe. Do you want me to send them on to you?
>
> Several people asked to be remembered to you – including Norman, Robert, Emma and Bob.
>
> Do please write if you can. Please. Give my regards to your mother.
>
>   Most sincerely,
>   St John'

Gradually you can ease back into the safety of anoymity and let the agonising moments seep away. No more letters. Not even a phone call. God is good. God is good.

Home. Home.

Quiet night, quiet stars, quiet sky, quiet earth; quiet, quiet, quiet. In the dull, matt finish of the furniture, in the opaque, white glow of the skirting board there is, he has found, solace. From his living room window he can see – it happens every night – a middle aged man undress. The man is huge, obese – so gross he's superb – and tonight is no exception. He watches the naked, fat man quiver out of his clothes, damp and warm from all that exertion. And this seems only to complete his happiness. Light spreading in pools across the sumptuous red glow of carpet, light shimmering up the smokey wallpaper, and a grey ceiling, and the ticking of clocks, a light drizzle murmuring in from the Atlantic, warmth and glorious peace of mind! His books with their gold lettering, the bell, the glasses, the decanters in ultramarine displayed with discretion, with careful disarrangement make this living room seem utterly perfect. His books lie against the wall possessing the worlds of art and history, photos of Persepolis and Timgad, Memphis and Rhodes, the

Temples of Luxor, the Colossi of Memnon, Italy in 1450, Savanarola and the stench of burning flesh, idylls and tortures and Malatesta at prayer, the Splendours of the Medici, the neuroses of the Tudors, Padua, Florence and Shakespeare at the Globe, Wilde being epigrammatic, Shaw being long-winded and Irish, the Nude, Dada, Surrealism and the Cubists – all on one shelf just below the cocktail cabinet.

Tonight is a night for legends, for drawing chairs closer to the hearth, listening to the fire spit, the creak of rosewood and stones smoothed away with years of rubbing. All those half-real, half-mystical things which scent the imagination.

Yet outside it's cold. A biting wind is blowing the pools of rain to and fro and couples are scurrying home to tea and soup. But it is impossible to feel downcast. Hot, brown cocoa in mugs smelling delicious, thick and sweet and sliding down a throat – and a moon! God, a white bright thing seen in countless movies, hanging above New England and Boston and the American Aristocracy, snow, moonlight in Vermont, sweet grass falling, falling stars way above the afterglow, mysterious taxis gliding in the warm dark night.

If I listen closely I can hear my heartbeat. If I'm quiet I can hear the clock. If I'm *very* still I can hear the silence filling the whole house.

Home. Home!

Desires rageing between the legs. But these are old vices.

At the back of the heart the small, still ache for vanished times, good times, the old days when you listened to the earth.

The croaking of tadpoles, white motes floating about the head and on the surface of the pond, waterflies skipping incessantly, pale weeds – chest high – waving in deep green slime on the river bank, and over everything a gentle somnolence – hot and hushed – below the swaying trees, in this Garden of Fand, pale faces quivering through the long grass and the rolling, golden wheat.

Home, home.

Part Two
LETTERS TO A FRIEND

Faroes.
Cromarty, Forth, Tyne.
Dogger, German Bight.
Rockall, Mallin, Hebrides.
Fastnet.

Once back home life slipped back into the pattern which had endured for so long – or so it seemed. Once back from London life resumed it's old pattern – on the surface. Downstairs into the melancholy house. 7.30 am. And the rain has fallen in torrents all night, down, over the house where we live – my family and I.

Sometimes – rarely – mum forgets to put the alarm on, then rushes downstairs, catching me sitting in the empty back kitchen and says,

'I'd have slept till the Lord called me, wouldn't I lad?' or 'We'd better get our skates on hadn't we?'

The grey light begins to lift. Rain blowing wildly in pools in the middle of the street. Somewhere the running sound of a distant tap – cold water drumming into a kettle, splashing down onto her plump hands.

Lift up your hearts quietly on the quiet radio.

Warsaw and Rabat,
Luxembourg and Limoges,
Athlone, Hilversum.

The Home,
The Light,
The Third.

(Nail varnish on the radiogram face so we can find where AFM is.)

And the house begins to stir into life. The grey light lifts and the rain ceases a little. The match is struck and the gas fire plops and hisses into life – warmth spreading from the calves to the backbone, mum bustling over toast, the tea made – she unbolts the front door and looks up and down the street, squinting through the rain, water on her forearms, sprinkling her soft pink skin – then, picking up the milk, she clicks the front door shut.

The lads begin to stir and wake. The girls cough out of bed. Mother standing in the long dark hall calling, 'Eileen! Maisie! Helen!' up the long, dark stairs, then she comes into the back kitchen smiling to me through the yellow toast-drenched light. The cool grey parlour and well kept linoleum. The rain sweeping in waves over the houses opposite. Flu in the bones.

Helen's overall (blue with chalk marks) bending down into the rain towards Carhartts at the end of the street. Maisie smelling of paint, off to Paton Calverts to make toy cars in bright red. Eileen – a waitress at the Nanking – in starched black and white, uniformed fresh from the Chinese laundry. Tony whistling to the docks, Kevin to the tea company, John to the bread factory.

Mum and I warm by the fire with potato cakes.

Nothing important happens here, nothing the world at large would consider, but it is the centre of our small universe, the small epic of a large family. A modest pageant.

But soon something subtle and disturbing. The faces at the door for the girls become regular faces, faces which form theselves into George and Dave and Tommy, and courtships are begun, and weddings are mentioned for the first time in our house. But they can't destroy what we have here. They *can't*. It's too precious to be replaced.

Even the lads form connections from which there is no escape – Frances and Jean and Rose and hurried conversations heard at night, in the parlour, voices raised in anger and other parents – neighbours from far Gloucester Place – shouting in the night.

'You've got to give your consent. You know what'll happen if you don't!'

Eileen outraged in the parlour, 'If he were my lad I'd say no!' but being mother she says yes to something, then comes to bed in tears.

Then John married Jean.

Giggling at the door one Saturday night, whispering voices on the other side of the vestibule, then Maisie bursts in with George announcing, 'We've got the ring mam!'

And all is light as we switch the radio off and handshakes are called for – Maisie who loved Nat King Cole and *When I Fall In Love It Will Be Forever*.

'I'd put it through his nose,' someone says, looking at the ring in it's white box, nestling in satin, and we laugh, and this time I think I understand.

Maisie married George.

Waking one night to tears in the next room. Kevin's voice shaking, cracked and different. I've never heard him cry before.

'I want to marry her mam, but I'm scared.' Then their voices drop back into tears and soft reassurances.

Weeks later Kevin married Frances.

And slowly the house empties and grows more silent –

especially on Fridays. Helen – cautious and self-conscious – abruptly says she has fallen for Tommy.

And she married him – white and virgin and covered in flowers.

Then Tony and gentle Rose.

And dread comes over me as the house echoes in the dark, as Fridays become as cold as Sundays.

Not Eileen.

NOT EILEEN!

But even she drifts away from us, even she goes. In a whirl the dress is bought, the ring chosen, the date set, as Suez smoulders in the East.

One day Eileen wed Dave – quietly at home.

And mother and I are left entirely, utterly alone. The house rattles and calls, the house with its rich, its voluptuous memories, crumbles into disrepair as the rats gnaw in the cellar and the distemper in the bare, empty rooms cracks, as blood-red bugs multiply and eat away the plaster, until the wooden ribs are exposed – picked clean as a bone and rotting into damp, moist ruin powdering our hair.

One by one they go. One by one the street empties as everyone is rehoused on vast estates circling the suburbs, one by one people – whom for years have been part of your life – go. One by one the houses fall into decay, one by one they crumble and disintergrate. Some of these people I shall never see again, some – glimpsed from the tops of buses in town, some half recognised in pubs, hesitatingly at the bar, in glasses. But most shall disappear.

People die or go away or succumb to illnesses in white circular wards.

Now even *things*, *objects* can no longer survive but disassemble, are blown away like smoke.

Farewell, a long farewell.

But I can hope, *I Can. I will*.

Scurrying, curling into history as his past tingles in a frail mist just below the eyes, just in front of the heart – heavy in the chest, as if he'd never been away, or aged, or grown so bitter. He fell into a constant looking back to a past which had never really existed, he fell into a constant dreaming in nostalgia which dulled the edge of failure.

Then a letter drops into the hall telling us that we are to be rehoused – as mother polishes the lavender linoleum, on her knees, backing down the hall towards the stairs.

In the clean new flat silence settles, thick as silt, as you wait for someone to come, for someone to ask you to go out, as you sit listening to the croak of doors from neighbours houses, sudden bangs, then more silence than you can bear, crushing down on you – this wretched Saturday evening.

Life slipped into a new order, a new pattern which was soon to become as familiar as the old one. Milk was delivered, people talked at doors, insurance money was placed on the radiogram, papers were bought from the man by the ferry, (*The Echo* during the week, *The Times* on Sundays), mum went to mass, meals were eaten in silence at regular times, he bathed twice a week, clothes were washed, suits bought at Christmas, buses caught – arriving at the office at 8.55 (9.30 if you overslept), every Friday, mum did the housework, every Friday, after work, he'd clean the windows, fix the curtains, fluff-up the cushions on the sofa, pull the hearth rug back an inch from the fireplace and adjust the discreet ornaments which she'd not replaced properly. Every Saturday he'd sleep in – waking at 1.00 to the smell of bacon and eggs, every Saturday the family would visit – grandchildren scattered through the flat at 4.00. Then early evening, pea soup, and mum dozing in front of the TV as the westerns drawled to a halt, a box of chocolates, cigarette ash on the floor, endless pots of tea. Sunday tomorrow – then work again, and the cushions needing refluffing, and the mat needing to be pulled back an inch from the hearth, and the hall needing to be swept of crisps and silver wrapping paper, and the traces of children.

Everything was just as it was – on the surface.

But just below the skin something was deeply wrong, just beneath the surface restraint was breaking down, the senses were exploding, the passions were being indulged, in a kind of sick ecstasy, made sick because it was hidden, because it came out only at night, as it dressed itself in leather and cowered in the dark.

I said I wouldn't go in.

I vowed it.

For months I'd resisted the temptation, then one day my resolution failed me and in an instant I was lost.

Sitting by the window with the bright, spring sunshine flooding down onto him as he softly strummed chords on a guitar. As his legs widened and his leather jeans stretched and squeaked as he shifted position, I went in. Nudity scattered about on the walls, stacked magazines with brown-thumbed edges. Quite sparse.

And he said, 'Hello'.

'They're a great pair of jeans,' I said now unable to control my shaking legs or my trembling voice. 'How much were they?'

'Twenty-six quid – made to measure,' he said as he got up and his thighs, his crutch seeming infinitely desirable.

'Have you got any books on leather?' I asked – quaking and horrified.

So much flesh, so much desirability. He walks towards me and stands looking through the stacks of magazines on a table at the back of the shop. I cannot take my eyes from his legs. He is so close.

'They're a great pair of jeans,' I say and my hand goes up and touches his buttocks.

'They're not worn in yet,' he says completely oblivious to my hand roaming over his rump. 'You've got to take them back after about three weeks to be taken in some more so that they're *really* tight.' And moves away to another pile of magazines.

Quaking in the silence, I simply watch him. He goes back to his seat, picks up his guitar, and opens his legs. We look at one another in the warm spring sunlight.

'Are you a leather guy?' I said after a long, *long* time.

'No.'

Warm spring silence.

Oh God have mercy on my thoughts.

His legs spreading wider and wider. I look at this crutch and imagine his cock.

'Can I feel you?' I say not knowing where I've found the courage or the desperation from.

'No.'

And my heart catching my throat.

'Pity,' shrugging my shoulders, trying to sound nonchalant.

How could I have said it? *How?* I stand there shocked into silence, appalled by my infinite lack of control.

'But if it's gay leather you're after I know someone who makes the more bizarre stuff.'

'How do I get in touch?'

'Through me. He's a customer. I'll ask him next time he's in – OK?'

'Thanks'.

'Cheers.' And he softly strums chords on his guitar.

I walk out – fallen and corrupt. How could I have said such things? How could I have behaved like that?

Yet next time it is easier and the time after that easier still until you feel, only occasionally, a shiver of shame on the back of the neck or a blush if women pass and see you walk out with your brown paper parcel. The young boy is not there on every visit. Sometimes it's a woman (then you don't buy anything) or a fat man with embarrassed eyebrows, and you even manage to joke with him as you point to a huge, ugly, veined penis and say, 'I wish mine was as big as that!' But usually there is that still quiet, as the few men move about the shop, cough, hover frightened-eyed over these explicit magaiznes, spend a fortune on five or six, then hurry away, crying out for anonymity and love and, of course, you can't have both.

After this initial baptism he will do *extraordinary* things. As if, as each humiliation becomes a habit, a new degradation must be sought as punishment, and as punishment turns into lust, as one sin compounds another, he will realise that the road to the gutter is long, that corruption knows no end and that you never touch bottom.

The long night of the soul was about to begin. The dark in the afternoon.

> LEATHER IS OUR BUSINESS!
> CHAINS, WHIPS, COLLARS, NOOSES, BALL WEIGHTS,
> COCK RINGS, SHACKLES – YOU NAME IT, WE'LL SUPPLY IT.
> IF YOU'RE A LEATHER GUY – YOU'LL NEED LEATHER,
> IF YOU NEED LEATHER – YOU'LL NEED US.
> WE'LL KIT YOU OUT, MAN.
> WE'LL MAKE YOUR LEATHER-LIFE *FUCKING*GOOD!

God have mercy.
Christ have mercy.

> MALEBOX SPECIAL – SEX DEVICES FOR THE SADOMASOCHIST
> – A GUIDE TO S & M LIVING –
> *PLAYROOM*: Many of our readers have written in to ask how to go about making a 'playroom' and how it should be equipped. Ideally it should be a cellar – then it'll have the right 'dungeon' atmosphere and this effect

can be heightened by bars over the windows and/or chains on the walls. But try to get a cellar with a high ceiling so that you'll be able to take a really good swing with a whip or a belt. If you can't get a cellar then an attic or box room will be better than nothing. You'll want it to be dark so paint the walls, ceiling, floors, doors black – this way if you're going to piss on someone (or for that matter if someone is going to piss on you) it won't show and besides black helps to hide the blood stains. What goes into a playroom depends entirely on you, but a rack is ideal (if you can afford to have one made that is) but ropes, chains, shackles and whips look good if prominently placed.

Listed below are a few of the finer accessories for those who take their S & M really seriously: . . .

Salvation through pain, seeking pain so that it might purify like a purging fire, the passion and the stake.

Chrome presses for crushing your victims testicles, renal catheters, arse-spreaders in (surgical steel), to be plunged into the rectum to squeeze it wider and wider, chastity belts to support the myth that your boy, your slave will be inviolate, whipping posts (simple wooden structures ideal for correction), cock rings and straps and sheaths to stretch, to pull the balls down to the kneecaps, harnesses, bondage collars, bit gags and locks to be inserted through holes pierced in the foreskin, earrings, restraining tables and hobble shackles, leather strait-jackets and hoods to entirely encase the head in leather, piss gags, bits, ball weights and branding irons, handcuffs, winches, racks and bondage boards, whips, arse plugs the size of truncheons, ropes, matches burning into the soft pink flesh of nipples and (most ironic of all) a cross.

Mea Culpa, Mea Culpa, Mea *Maxima* Culpa.

Through my fault, through my fault, through my most grievous fault.

MALEBOX TRADE:
Attractive blonde sun-worshipper. Handsome 6'2" sensual male looking for kindred spirit. Behind this box number is a together man . . .

Americans with huge bodies Frenchmen with small, chic lusts, but oceans of embarrassed Englishmen juggling with their genteel, seedy desires.

Muscular leather guy into S/M in the market for slave – Are you well built, well-hung and looking for an obedient leather boy – I'm a sucker for active leathermen with big tits – Pleased to oblige – Am willing to learn – Really beautiful stripped – 36 yr old available for dominant leather/denim stud – Handsome guy into tight jeans would like to hear from young men in need of discipline – Mud wrestler requires patch – Are you into wellies? – Does the idea of leather shorts and oil turn you on – I'm looking for a lasting sincere relationship – A youngish 40 – A youthful 50 –

Discreet of Salisbury, Anxious of Cheltenham, Guiness in Swansea, Rubber in Llanelly, Cultured of Gloucester, Charming of North Devon, Considerate in Sussex and Average of Bromley.

Medway, Maidstone, Berkshire and Sheffield. Anyone in Manchester, Oxfordshire students, Andy of Koblenz, Deaf gays in Hastings, Someone in Cardiff. Lonely of Hants, Genuine of Cornwall, Cuddly midgets from Central London and aching graduates bleating from Anglesea.

All cry out, in small cold print across pages, acres of adverts on glossy paper: All letters answered – Photo essential

– Telephone number ensures quick reply – No camps – No kinks – No bags – No dice.

Carlisle, Ashford, Birmingham, Notts, Belgium, Denmark, Holland, Japan, St Albans, Reading, Chester and Grimsby, Husky of Brighton, Luton and the South-East, Goodlooking of Wanstead, Nimble of Esher, Plymouth and Weston-Super-Mare, Youthful of Aberdeen, Mid-thirties of Kent, Bisexual Scotsmen lusting in kilts, Jamacian corset queens sipping Bacardi, Camp Chinese houseboys into rubber and Wagner. And where is the gay community of Crouch End? And Wicked Enfield, and Sinful, Tempting Potters Bar.

Am I the only MALEBOX reader who enjoys plastic baby pants?

He read and re-read the adverts until he knew them off by heart, until they made him claw and crave and long for ecstasy.

For a second time he begins to write and hope.
Young man. Young man wants. Young man wants leather guy. Young man wants leather guy for corporal punishment. And strict training.

'Leicester
My preferences are easy. I like *long* sessions, lasting all night if possible, but I realise that with two of us this would be impossible. So I always indulge in threes – as it gives more excitement and longer workouts. I'm sorry you don't want a trio but I wasn't clear in my meaning – you think it would be difficult to serve two masters and you are right . . .'

Am very obedient. Am very obedient and willing to learn.

'Copenhagen
Right you were – I am a master – yes your future master! I dig

the idea of large tattoos. When I like tattoos – you of course WILL also like them. I have got 16 inch biceps and big tits (which I am wild to have sucked!). I want my tits and upper arms tattooed – like the Angels in Los Angeles – or do you think it showier anywhere else?'

I am 5'7". I am 5' 7" and have blue eyes. I am 5' 7" and have blue eys and dark hair. I am 30 years of age – and slim.

' . . . however, with me, there is only one master and everyone else is a slave. I merely make one slave use, abuse and degrade the other whilst I watch them and see that my orders are carried out. Each person serves only ME.'

Long powerful strokes on tender flesh.

'I want you tattooed with my symbol . . .

and I want it on your left tit!'

Studs – in intricate designs – covering his body harness.

'I prefer the two slave arrangement because I have found it easier when breaking-in a new slave – by observing his fellow slave it helps him grasp the finer points of his master's personality and it removes the embarrassment of asking or error – both of which ruin the effect. Even though you are miles away you can be as frequent a slave here as others. This is my idea of permanence. How does it strike you?'

The swastika. The eagle.

'I know a young muscular guy on whose entire back is an eagle and Nazi insignia – oh so thrilling!'

The leather tendrils of the leather lash.

'I will expect you to be totally obedient in every respect. You will be submissive from the moment we meet and give up all rights and privileges to your own views. You will be punished for every fault whether it is real or not and without regard for justice or fact. That puts you in the picture as to your treatment.'

The soft caress. The round, the yielding flesh.

'I want a letter from you telling me how wonderful I will look tattooed and a description of where you want my body tattooed and what the tattoos will consist of. Indeed a whole rambling page on this matter is required.'

A tender whipping. The creak and stretch of limbs.

'Fill out the form enclosed. The next week will pass quickly so get into shape for some real subservience. You will need to be very fit and healthy, because my sessions go on for hours and you may be awake all evening, even all weekend.'

Thinking of an excuse to get to Leicester yet knowing I'll never venture further than a wet dream.

'Your tattoo description was insufficient! I *command* you to tell me where you want your master's body to be tattooed and what you want the tattoos to be like. A WHOLE DESCRIPTION IS NEEDED! You MUST make four detailed drawings showing what you want on my tits, back, biceps and my cock and balls. Answer me! This dominator of yours!'

'Your deliberate disobedience in not complying with my wishes by filling out your personal measurement check-list is an obvious show of your need for correction. It shall be done until you are truely repentant. Your worthless body shall be punished. Punishment is not reserved for errors or mistakes, sadism is for the unjust and deliberate degradation of the slave who is penalised for doing well, for obedience and service, to show him that he will always be a subservient nothing. You will sort out your tightest clothes. During the train journey and throughout your visit you will wear no underwear except for your cock and ball strap which you will not remove however sore your bollocks become. It is to become a part of you. The following instructions are my final ones and you will obey them'

'Disobedient bastard! Is your cunt-brain too small!? I am going to rip your tits off for not carrying out my orders! I'm going to string you up by your balls! I want a description of the tattoos you want on me. I WANT! I WANT! You shall be strung up and your body hair removed – dog you *dig* that? You poor but D E A R slave. From your master in black leather with big tits!
    Torben.'

'. . . you will address all your future letters to 'Dear Master' and sign yourself 'Obedient Slave'.

'Prepare your worthless body and make it ready for use. Your visit will be fulfilling – the fulfillment of obeying all my wishes as my slave. Be prompt. I don't like to be kept waiting. Obey.
    Roy.'

No replies from Denmark. No replies from Leicester. Such is the cost of disobedience.

'Dear Friend,
I am writing in reply to your recent advertisement in MALEBOX . . . '

'Dear Young Leatherman,
Thank you for your strong interest in my ad. I am a farmer . . .'

42 – too old.

'. . . my interest in leather is different, only mildly S/M. I enclose 4 photos of myself in leather.
        Eero, Finland.'

Dear Friend,
I saw your advert in MALEBOX and decided to reply.

'Hello Liverpudlian! Thanks for the reply to my ad. I was away on holiday touring Lapland and Russia. Well I am 32, a Swede living in Norway. I am tall, some 6 feet, rather well built, strong and masculine. Got a BMW bike and am very keen on leather and everything connected with it . . .'

Rubber clothing and sado-masochism.

' . . . there are of course many ways of degradation and torture and I like them all . . . '

His English is very good.

' . . . I like to get my victim completely down, whip him until he gets soft, piss all over him or into his mouth, then really go to work on him . . . '

Thanks for your letter. I hope you enjoyed your holiday. It sounded great.

'. . . I like then to go on with the torture using every part of my victims body. I go on for as long as I enjoy it. And that's mostly for a very long time. Write a longer letter letting me know your likes and dislikes as well as your experiences. Send a photo too. All the best,
    Michael, Denmark.'

Hi Mike, did you get my last two letters? Sorry I didn't send a photo but I don't have one at the moment.

Hello! Did you get my last letter? I've sent several over the last three weeks but as I've not heard from you I thought I'd drop you a line.

I'd like to know more about you so will you please write soon?

Please. Will you? Will you write? It'd be great if we could meet. Wouldn't it? Hey? I'm really keen. Honest.

'Hello boy, you are first English person with courage enough to confess at once his deepest personal desire. If I am first leather man what you are choose helping your problems I feel strongly my responsibility. Well I like continue correspondence with you.'

Lots of discipline.

'. . . if you have nude photo of you I hope see it, so I can imagine better how manipulate and punish you when (or if) we meet . . .'

(But I *want* Michael!)

'. . . our summer is very bad, because weather disturb harvesting. It is rainy day again and I have little time for correspondence. I hope you understand. I have more time after 20th September. Hoping hear from you again.,
    Eero'

Exhilarated by sadism.

There's a picture (that of an American wrestler taken immediatley after his bout). Only one eye is open and the rest of his face is covered in sweat and blood. His front teeth and tongue are smudged with blood and saliva. Folds of skin – from the neck to the chest – are dark, almost black with blood. And through all that torn inflamed flesh he is smiling.

Batter my heart three-person'd God.

'Hello Boy, thank you for your letter. You seem to be boy of large dimensions of life. Your letter explain many new things about you and base of your sexuality. Because you have drop of poet in your blood, your phantasies are violent. Perhaps reality – when you find guy to punish and 'use' you – make you frustration: behind curtain you find another truth – majority of leather men are mother-controlled, some love closely. Son angry mother dominant. My mother is strongly dominant. We have often abnormally strong sexual potency and this makes us regular masturbator or 'leather hungry'. Leather thus become our way express our sexuality . . . '

It's good to have someone to talk to.

'. . . unfortunately I am not so brutal manly 'bear' you need, but I have hairy peasant body with smell of sweat, warm blood and heart . . . '

Michael! Michael!

Dear Eero.

'. . . remember in phantasies we can make up very fine image for our deepest desire but in cold reality is often big unsuccess. We still dream of leather phantasies but find only depression. I know. I am tortured too much myself with them many, many years . . . '

Hungry for a leather man.

'. . . we have some days still for harvesting and I have not time for writing.'

He seems a kind man.

'. . . you try to get out of your prison but 'freedom' is big risk . . . danger . . . '

The fly. The cock.
Slipping into indifference.

'. . . I am tired after hard days of potato harvesting so hot sauna bath after this. I hope next time I can write more exciting things to you . . . '

Writing to other advertisements. Placing my own. Waiting for the replies to trickle in.

'. . . write soon boy if you find time.

      Eero.'

Finland seeming very far away.
Dear Master. Dear Friend. Dear Santa Claus.

> MALEBOX SURGERY:
> Dear Doctor, what are the benefits (or otherwise) of cock-rings?
> Dear Doctor, can I get internal injuries through being beaten?

Dear Doctor, do weights hung on the balls cause any permanent damage?
Dear Doctor, I am interested in cock-tattooing and wish to have this done. Is it harmful?

Dear Doctor is there any remedy for *my* ailment?
Dear Doctor can you *cure* the sick?

Dear Doctor, I'm really into pierced nipples and love the idea of an erectile tit with a steel pin or ring through it. In fact I've just had my own tits pierced and love to fondle the rings and spikes through this part of my hairy chest. Can you assure me that this type of piercing is harmless?

'You want your *what* pierced?' Barely audible in the long jewellers shop.

'My nipples,' low over the high counter.

'We only do ears sir.'

Expensive soft silence as I change feet, cough then sink deeper into the carpet. 'You won't do it for me then?' As the elderly assistant fidgets behind the engagement rings.

'I'm sorry, sir, but the gun is designed only for ears – *Ears.*'

And we both go red.

MALEBOX DOCTOR REPLIES TO YOUR LETTERS:
Dear Reader, I see no reason why you shouldn't have your nipples pierced.
Dear Reader, there aren't any specific risks attached to cock-tattooing (except the risk of local skin infection) but I do hear that it is exquisitely painful. So find a reputable tattooist. What design did you have in mind? Why not write in fellas, and tell us of *YOUR* rare or unusual cock-tattoos?

The dial tone. The pips. The terrible waiting and the churning in the bowels, then a tattooed voice growls into the mouthpiece. 'Jacks!'

Waiting unable to speak.

'Is that the tattooist?'

'Yer.'

'I, er, I want my bollocks tattooed.'

A terrible waiting.

'I won't touch a prick for less than twenty notes.'

Aching – aching.

'Will you do it?'

'It takes a hell of a fucking time. I've got a tattoo on my own chopper and it took me three days to get it on. Besides it hurts like fuck.'

Desperate – desperate.

'Will you do it?'

'Apart from the time it takes it's gotta be hard as a biscuit – you'll be wankin' off by the minutes.'

A terrible craving. Silence as the telephone wires crackle then die. Please say you'll do it! *Please*.

'What do you want on it anyway?'

A ray of hope.

'I want "fuck" down the back of my cock and a swastika on each of my balls.'

Silence. Will he do it?

'Will you?'

'Well . . . I mean . . . you might have a dose and I've got it in me hand, I do it for you then three weeks later I'm scratching the bollocks off meself.'

'You won't get a dose off me.'

'Yer – that's what they all say when they come in here and a lot of guys want their bollocks tattooed.'

'Will you do it?'

'It's no skin off my fucking nose. But It'll cost you. If I hold a prick in my hand I want payin' – thirty notes no messin!'

I can't afford so much. A long, a terrifying pause.
'When can I come round?'
'No – I won't touch a prick for less than fifty . . . '
And then the line goes dead.

> *Let him kiss me with the kisses of his mouth,*
> *For thy love is better than wine.*
> *Tell me. O thou whom my soul loveth.*

What do you want me to say? What do you want me to be as I sit here on the edge of your bed kissing your belly?

> *Behold thou art fair, my love,*
> *Behold thou art fair.*

What do you *want*? Nothing I can give as he tells me that he's a non-fucking, non-kissing, passive pederast. He even shows me photographs of grinning, self-confident youths whom he 'has' regularly, who look like football supporters or attenders of technical colleges.

> *Thou hast dove's eyes, Thy cheeks are*
> *comely, thou art all fair, my love,*
> *Thou hast ravished my heart,*
> *Thy lips drop as the honeycomb.*
> *Thy navel, thy breasts, thy neck, thy lips.*

Yet he seemed so perfect in the empty public lavatory, in the potent dark, with his beard and his Grecian thighs, in the short journey to his flat, in the cab, as he looked me up and down. Even now as I suck, as I claw at his rump, he screws his buttocks together, then thrusts at me, hands on hips, grunting, trying to prevent softness.

> *His legs are pillars of marble,*

> *His mouth is most sweet,*
> *Yea he is altogether lovely.*

'Do you like it? Do you think I've got a big cock?' he says – low and abashed – as the hoped-for, longed-for erection does not come, as I suck more frantically than ever. He takes it from my mouth, trying to shake it into hardness. Then slides it back in again. But it's no good.

> *Behold, thou art fair, my beloved, yea pleasant.*
> *A bundle of myrrh is my beloved, my beloved*
> *is unto me as a cluster of camphire in the*
> *vineyards of En-Gedi.*
> *This is my beloved, and this is my friend,*
> *O Daughters of Jerusalem.*

'It's not very successful is it?'
'No, he says, 'I thought *you'd* have a bigger cock than that.'
'I'm sorry,' I said feeling peeved, 'But there's nothing I can do about that. What a pity I'm not seventeen.' Then back to my lollipop. And he actually laughed, then threw a dressing gown over his pink, manly nakedness and I called him 'kid' and could've fallen for him – given time.

> *He shall lie all night betwixt my breasts.*

'I dig the leather though,' he says, 'how long have you been wearing it?' And for the first time I don't feel embarrassed or ashamed. In fact I feel slightly amused. 'About a year,' I say and conscious of my aching feet, dreading the walk home.

> *He brought me into the banqueting-house,*
> *and his banner over me was love. I sat*
> *down under his shadow with great delight.*

*His left hand is under my head, and his
right hand doth embrace me.*

Years will pass, then one evening by the fire, or in a room, or at a door, a smell will come, like an arm lifted, and there will be – just for a second – that vision of that man with a beard and good thighs who flung himself on a bed. All pink, all naked, wanting to be loved – who stood hands on hips, and the taste of him in your mouth. You will remember that night – how the sudden summer cold bit into your hands, how his hard man's arse – tight as fire – convulsed under your hands as he thrust and thrust towards you, deeper and deeper into your throat and how, after failing to satisfy either him or yourself, he told you that he was a car dealer.

*If two lie together then they have heat;
But how can one be warm alone?
And woe unto him that is alone when he falleth.*

Then home. And the empty taxi cabs. The darkened shop fronts and the small, expanding fear that mother might have woken, got up to use the toilet, and calling downstairs and not hearing you answer, inching down, trembling and bewildered and, finding you absent, waiting for you in the living room.

'Where have you been?' Then, 'What are you dressed like that for?' in shocked embarrassment.

But luckily, no, she didn't wake. Quietly you put key to lock and squeaked in. Quietly you undressed then hid your fetish. Quietly you coughed then made cocoa with a clatter. And no one was any the wiser.

You clever bastard, you naughty, *naughty* boy.

For weeks – even months – you're free of it, free from temptation. Then one day, one night, you see an arm, a chest, an arse and it all starts again – that dull ache, that old fire. The vision of God seen for a fleeting second. Flesh trapped inside beige leather pants and tight, *tight* T-shirts.

> *I rose to open to my beloved, I opened to*
> *my beloved but my beloved had withdrawn*
> *himself and was gone. My soul failed. I*
> *sought him but I could not find him. I*
> *called him but he gave me no answer. By night*
> *on my bed I sought him whom my soul loveth,*
> *I sought him but I found him not.*

Then one day, one *night*, as I was revisiting that wrecked landscape where my childhood and happiness died so long ago, as I walked through Brougham Terrace, the underground toilets were spread out before me, quivering under shrubbery – tantalising. Powerless to resist I drop below ground level and watchful, greedy eyes drop below my waistline. That male smell stinging the nostrils.

Leaving all hope behind – I had entered the cottage industry.

> *I will rise now and go about the city in the*
> *streets and in the broad ways. I will seek*
> *him whom my soul loveth.*
> *I sought him but I found him not.*

Standing in the lavatories thinking, 'They raided this cottage last Thursday – what would I do if I were arrested?'

> *The watchmen that go about the city – all*
> *hold swords, being expert in war, every man*
> *hath his sword upon his thigh because of fear*
> *in the night.*

Agents provocateurs.

> *The watchmen that go about the city*
> *found me, they smote me, they wounded*
> *me.*
> *I passed from them.*

Pushing my hand away from his cock, 'You dirty cunt!', and I wait for the next man to come in.

> *Whither is my beloved gone?*

Then in he comes overweight and black and I quiver in the tingling dark.

> *I went down into the garden.*
> *I found him whom my soul loveth!*
> *I held him and would not let him go!*

I was obliged to go in by the back door. Into the quiet, ticking room with two alabaster dogs – astonished on the sideboard. A doll's house. Small-talk crumbling into silence.
'D'you wanna go up?'
'Aye. OK.'
Handprints on the wallpaper up the stairs, dirty towels draped along the bannister. Lying in this ugly, little room, grunting under a hot, sweltering quilt, his breath tasting of cigarettes, his mouth smelling of fluoride toothpaste, running my hands down over his shoulders to the buttocks then recoiling as soft piles (round as grapes) cling to the fingertips, wet skin clapping on wet skin, rivers of sweat running into the hair making it limp and sag.

Dogs yelping tentatively at one another in the yard. Dear God how can I be doing this at my age? Dogs mounting one another in the street as passive, as expressionless as Elizabethans. His sperm splashing over my arms and belly. Washing in the small, over-decorated bathroom, the desire to penetrate, or to be penetrated, the desire to splash yourself over the whole world.

> *Who is this that cometh out of the*
> *wilderness like pillars of smoke?*
> *Who is she that looketh forth as the*
> *morning, fair as the moon, clear as the*
> *sun and terrible as an army with banners?*

'Can I see you again?' Hoping he'll say yes.
'Well . . . er . . . no – I'm married pal.'
'Oh.'

> *What will ye see in the Shulamite?*
> *She is the only one, she is the choice*
> *one, he saw her and blessed her, yea*
> *praised her.*

'Cheers!'
'See yer.' As I'm politely shown the door.

> *Love is strong as death, jealousy is*
> *cruel as the grave, the coals thereof*
> *are coals of fire which hath a most*
> *vehement flame. Many waters cannot*
> *quench love neither can floods drown it.*
> *Turn away thine eyes from me for they have*
> *overcome me.*

Out past the chapel in Jubilee Drive.

> *His left hand should be under my head*
> *and his right hand should embrace me!*

Christ is risen – salvation is at hand! And the empty park,

the cars drifting noiselessly towards town, the feet aching, the heart heavy as you tread over soft asphalt, swinging left past the dancehall with groups of young men (in white T-shirts with those cap-sleeves) spinning along, their gorgeous young arms exposed and thrilling. Young. YOUNG.

They are dreams incarnate, they are carnality made whole until all the young men you'd ever dreamt of blur, merge into one composite, virile, sex-drenched, gorgeous male – one face, one flesh, one body, no mind to speak of just a vast appetite, an ageless, an insatiable potency, like in myth, like in legend. The folklore of sex.

'L'Pool
Lunchtime.

I
L O V E
Y O U !

Billy
xxx
(Will write longer tonight)
PS- Some say start in a cottage – end in a cottage, but I don't think that's true of us, do you darling?
Billy xxx
PPS-Isn't it daft you not knowing my surname?
Billy xxx.'

It seems as though we spend our lives making love in wretched rooms with men too lonely or too insensible to care.

'Lunchtime
Hello Darling,
Thank you for two wonderful days, I did enjoy them. I'm

looking forward to Friday so that I can bring all my senses into play when we meet. Mum says of course you could stay, and what am I asking for and what does he eat and he looks so thin, needs someone to look after him and shouldn't be on his own. God she's so camp at times!

How's *your* mum love? Feeling better? Did you go to the doctor's? Bet you didn't. I love you and missed you so much today – especially at work. Malcolm was there but it didn't upset me too much. He said 'Hello, how are you,' and that was about it. I let that one know that she can't hurt me again – now that I have you. To think I tried to kill myself because of her.

I know it's daft writing to you when I only live a bus ride away but I just can't help myself. Love you! Love you! Love you!'

Drawling through booze 'ILUVYER' in a black-and-tan voice, feeling his warm slightly damp skin against me, feeling his warm slightly damp genitals and the heavy belly, and his back, his buttocks, his legs, tasting his after-shave – and his boyish smile.

'Darling,

I'm sorry that I wasn't in when you called to the house and that you'd had to phone repeatedly but I didn't get in until after 1.00am. I had to do a late job (with Malcolm of all people!) I should've left a message. Please forgive my callousness. I'll try to be in next time you come.

Goodnight my love.
    Billy xxx'

Licking then pushing his thick finger into my anus, hurting me, then the flagging erections, then the silence and breath condensing on the window panes. Strip lighting over the white bedroom unit mirror. A day's growth on my chin.

'I've got to go.'
'Pleesestay.'
'I've got to go.'
'Goodnightgobless.' Then snoring fitfully into incomprehensibility, shaking his thick penis into slow, fading action. Fumbling downstairs, in the dark finding the door (usually the back one) and leaving.

'Oh Darling,
Although busy over the weekend you have never been very far away from my thoughts. I love you very much – *Partir c'est mourir un peu*, to part is to die a little – how very true that saying is at times, darling, especially after out little misunderstanding over Malcolm.
Still love me? Even after last night?
You made me realise how thoughtless I can be at times and I do apologise (again) for misleading you.'

And second thoughts *creeping* in – along with replies to my last advertisement. M of Chipping Camden, Robin, Brian, George and Frank. And Guy who has a tremendous penchant for Czech music and leather and, although he lives in Beckenham, once visited Prague, and who urges me to get to know Janacek.

'So Darling, it was back to the grind this morning and guess what? That's right – I've got his lordship working with me. *Again*. But I'll survive. I think that of the two of us, he is the one who is more embarrassed and uncomfortable. (After all *he* did ditch *me*). But, at times, the situation is quite good, sweet even. It's much better to be civilised about it and watch them squirm after.
A feeling of revenge I suppose.'

Marc from London who's short but fairly versatile – 'Don't

think one can generalise over sex really. It depends so much on circumstances, partner and so on. Don't go much on pubs and clubs and I'm certainly no 'cottage crawler'. Still being so near to London you don't need to be. Just keep your eye open and seize the opportunities when they arise. And they sure do, believe me. (Apart from Berlin – which is fabulous – London is the best place in Europe, in my experience.)'

'Dearest, dearest Caution,
Thank you for your letter. I do apologise for not answering it before now and I hope I haven't caused you any pain or anxiety. Right this minute I need you more than you will ever know – emotionally more than physically. Think of me. I *will* post this letter right away so you shall get it Thursday morning perhaps . . .'

'No,' says Steve of Chelmsford, 'I think the ideal gear is skin tight jeans (with nowt on underneath) or tight leather jeans with a jock-strap or briefs, boots, leather jacket, studded wrist straps, studded belt (3" wide) and a leather vest or T-shirt and a big heavy collar for the neck (I wear a padlock on mine which is really sexy!)'

'. . . phone me on Thursday night love at about 7 o'clock and we can talk about it to –'

'What's the sex life up in the Pool like,' asks John in Kent, 'or do you go to Manchester which I hear isn't bad?'

'–gether. Tonight is the first time since last I saw you that I've had more than ½ an hour to myself. As you know on Friday I was at my coven (in Greater Manchester), and the festivities went on until Saturday evening. I got home about 9.30 pm on Sunday and went straight to bed absolutely exhausted. Then after a couple of hours sleep I had to get up

and go out on a job – that's why you weren't able to get hold of me. So I do hope you will forgive me. I love you and *only* you.
Billy xxx.'

Crabs and the end of the air. The rotteness at the core of man. The black Narcissus.

'I've got to go . . .'
'Goonight . . . gobles . . .'

> *And his fruit was sweet to my taste.*
> *For I am sick with love.*

And waiting in the wings. Tony (Dublin), Sven (on Malta), Stuart in Nottingham and Uncle Ted Willis and all.

'Three weeks in Cyprus – business *and* pleasure (lucky men!)'
'Urine drinking – from which I get great pleasure.'
'Dark and tanned.'
'Keen on denim.'
'Hot wild sex . . .'
'Faded jeans and jacket.'
'Quite well built.

And so the litany goes on. So the chant continues.

'Can't put you up – I share a flat.'
'Would love to meet but just like you I too am passive.'
'Keep in trim.'
'Am forty-four.'

Yet you keep on writing, keep on hoping that one day your prince will come. Paratroopers who live in Central

London, athletic dancers in SW3 who like being slapped around, thirty-seven year olds who are passive but own their own flats.

'Glasgow

Dear box 17/104,

Hello Friend, Pardon the formality but after all you didn't tell me your first name.

I am thirty one. medium-slim build, fairish hair, about 5' 8" or 9". I like modern clothes, good quality films and music. My hobbies are photography, motoring and sex. (Not necessarily in that order!) But I go *mad* over leather. (I play chess as well – is there no end to this kid's versatility?).

I am very broadminded so if there are any questions you want to ask in your reply, please do.

I hope that my sense of humour comes through this letter – up here you've got to see the funny side of things or you'd go mad.

So write soon with lots more details – sordid or otherwise! (My grammar is ruined by exclamation marks!) Also send a photo if you have one. I enclose the one and only picture of myself so I hope you fancy me from it.

      Yours,
           Iain.'

I'm thirty-three, slim, dark hair.

'Dear Robbie,

Thanks for your letter all too brief though it was. Unfortunately, although I love leather, I don't own as much as you do – a leather jacket is all I can boast I'm afraid. However I can't wait to see some pictures of you in your complete outfit. Jesus all that leather! So send me some more pix as soon as you get them. I only wish I was the photographer taking them.

Sure I like to suck cock – like giving it as well. We'll likely get on fine. As for the sado-masochistic stuff – well I'm all for it. Usually I prefer being dominant but I'm very adaptable and like doing ANYTHING provided I do it with leather. But I LOVE my arse being licked out – don't like doing it – but I love someone doing it to me. How about you? Maybe you'll tell me in your next letter just what specifically you like and what you don't like. Let me know in more detail also what other kinds of deviations or kinks you enjoy. I seem to be asking a helluva lot of questions so if you want to ask me any go right ahead and ask them.

I think it is far better being completely frank from the start, don't you?

So please write soon.
      Yours,
         Iain,'

If, after seeing the snaps, you lose interest don't be afraid to say so will you?

'Monday

Dear Robbie,

Thanks for your letter and the photographs. They're not as sexy as I'd have liked. However if and when we meet I'll take some really sexy shots of you in (and out) of your leather gear. I was wondering if you went to a studio to get them done or did a friend take them? They appear to have been taken by a competent photographer but the pieces of furniture in them made me have second thoughts –'

Sitting naked – side-ways-on to the camera and tripod – then kneeling up on the couch, so that my genitals lie passive between my thighs, the photographer puts a black sheet up behind me making my white skin seem even whiter; then he slides his rough ringed left hand over my shoulders then down towards the soles of my feet, which are curled under me, grubby from the coconut matting on the floor. He looks at me and smiles then his right hand cradles my bollocks and pushes them further between my thighs and he says, still smiling, 'Have you gone soft then?'

'– talking about meeting each other I will be on a weeks holiday as from Saturday November 15th. I'm going to visit friends in London (gay of course!) but if you have a place of your own or any other ideas, as I have a car, I could come back from London via Liverpool –'

Don't give everything to those guys in London. Save something for the provinces and the underprivileged.

'Now turn towards the camera and open your legs.'
And, still naked, still kneeling – I do so. The round hot lights burn behind the tripod. He pops up from behind the lens cap and I start to go hard.

'– I really would love to photograph you in all that leather gear, your leather jacket open (with your nipples exposed) and with your leather jeans open, your bollocks hanging out –'

'Now the rising sun.' And I get off the couch, turn my back towards the camera in order to show my thin, white buttocks.

'– I'd also love a shot of you with a really big hard-on! Maybe you'd like to take some of me? Let me know any ideas you have in your next letter –'

He comes out from behind the camera and turns me right round. His right hand gripping then running up and down the entire shaft of my penis.

'Now one of the John Thomas?' Nodding I open my legs wide and he brings the camera down to crutch level.

The lights burn and I throb towards seven hard inches, he clicks away trying to banter, trying to sound bland and indifferent.

'– I think I've already told you of my likes and dislikes as far as sex is concerned. I like anything. I prefer being the dominant partner – and then I'll do anything. But most of all I adore fucking. (I don't mind being fucked as long as it doesn't prove too painful). But the thought of spunking into your mouth and all over your face is just fantastic! I've got a boner just thinking about it! –'

Self-consciously getting into my leather pants and pushing it down one leg, balls down the other.

'Leave the top of your jeans turned back and the fly open all the way down. That'll give you definition.'

And the black hairs running from navel to pubis.

'– You may have gathered by now that I'm a bit of a randy bastard – in the nicest possible way of course. Not that I see anything wrong with that – it's just frustrating when I get to know someone like you who lives so far away –'

The lights are now so hot I'm sweating inside my leathers. I pull on the boots, tucking my leather jeans into them. I pull on my leather shirt and jacket and water runs down the nape of my neck, along my spine.

'Now pull the motorcycle cap down over your eyes and put your sun-glasses on.'

I do so.

'Open your legs.'

I do so.

'Now put your hand between them – very nice.'

'– Let me know in your next letter what you want me to do to you and if we can meet. But please be specific about your preferences as it makes me randy to read about these things –'

Undressing then packing my leather gear into an overnight bag.
'When will they be ready?'
'Oh – about Tuesday.'
'Shall I pay now or when I call for them?'
'Oh when you collect them will be fine.'
But I leave a deposit of one pound all the same.
'Cheers.'
'Bye.'
And out past the wedding photographs.

'– By the way could I contact you perhaps by phone? I myself don't have one but I could phone you from the office almost any night provided you can give me a number. But don't go spending a fortune phoning me when I can phone you for nothing.
Well Robbie, write as long and as sexy a letter as you can. I'll be waiting for it.
   Yours,
    Iain.'

He seems so promising.

           'Thursday
Dear R,
Well it was really great to speak with you on the phone last night. I think you've got a very sexy voice and a great accent. You also sounded really sensible (don't ask me how I come to think that!)

The more I think of it, the more it seems too good to be true – us getting to know each other. We seem to like to do the same things – sex wise, anyway. And I think that's more than half the battle. Because if you don't get on too well with one another sexually there's nothing much either can do. You can't change your sex likes when you want. They're just there. The rest can come through time but I think sexual fulfillment is the most important aspect. Anyway enough of my philosophies.

I've managed to put by fifteen rolls of film for my holidays so, with twelve pictures to each roll, I'm planning to take more than just a couple of pictures of you. More like a couple of hundred. Christ I can't wait! The Friday, Saturday and Sunday will be a lifetime too short for me. Still it will have to do.

Anyway, sexy, I'll be looking forward to your letter before I go on holiday, and LIVING for a week on Friday 8.00 pm. So take care of yourself till then.

       Love

          Iain, xxx.'

Please let this be it because need is greater than fear.

                            'Thursday/Friday.

Well, believe it or not, this letter is from me. I'm working what is known in the office as 'the late, late show' – which means I start work at 6.30 pm on Thursday night and don't finish until 3.30 am on Friday morning. Terrible isn't it? I don't do this shift very often but this week the one or two people who usually do it are off ill, so here I am. I've run out of reading material so I've chosen YOU to write to – out of dozens of prospective recipients – my sense of humour deteriorates as the night goes on, as you will gather.

It is now 1.00 am Friday morning and one of the office copy-boys has just brought me a cup of tea. It's more like something they surface roads with but, at least, it's hot and wet. (The tea I mean!) I'm not keeping you awake am I? Anyway. Getting back to the copy-boys. There's one in particular and I'm certain he's gay. He dresses really sexy and isn't bad looking. Everytime he passes me he usually looks but it's not just an ordinary, everyday look – it lasts just-that-bit-longer-than-usual and, as I say, it's infuriating not being certain if he's gay. Maybe he thinks the same thing, I don't know. He came in one day last week with a see-through shirt on and, quite honestly, I couldn't keep my eyes off him. I think he must have gathered then that I was watching him every time he passed. Still, there's hope yet.

Well – on to other things Carruthers!

The gay life up here is pretty awful. It's only once in a blue moon that I meet someone who goes in for leather and the really kinky stuff. Mostly they are just everyday gay guys which bores me after a time. So when I was down in England some time ago I got a copy of MALEBOX and put in the ad. Thank God it paid off. (That copy-boy is staring at me again, I think I'll go over and rape him.)

You say you live with just your mother. I live with my father but, as I work peculiar shifts and he works a normal 9 to 5, we don't see each other too often. I have every morning off and usually about three or four nights free a week. As I work part-time in a photographers studio in the mornings it breaks the monotony, an I usually try to coax someone back to my house and take some pix of them or something (no prizes for guessing what that 'something' might include!!)

Well, Rob, I'd better go and socialise with some of the other chaps in the office or they'll think I've turned into a recluse or something. But do write and make it long and sexy.

      Iain xxxx.'

His breath will smell of smoke, his brown body will be

hard to the touch, and you will tell him that you love him.

'Well Buddy Boy,

I just wish I were getting all these letters! I suppose I just like writing them (Or had you guessed that by now?)

I hope, thinking back, that I didn't give you the impression on the phone the other night that I wasn't keen on our relationship getting serious, that it was just for sex. It's just that I had an 'affair' some time ago and, when we broke up, I was really upset and so was my 'affair'. We still see each other though. We're still friends.

However I really long for another relationship, and the feeling of security and all that goes with it. But I'd have to be really sure that it would work. What broke up my last affair was the fact that I wasn't being satisfied sexually. We had the usual sex alright and we both enjoyed it but that was all. As you know I like being dominant and piss-fun and the like but unfortunately my boyfriend didn't. And, as I have said, sexual fulfillment is the most important thing. The rest can come in time. So that's me in the old proverbial nutshell!

Well, babe, less than a week to go before we meet. Just think of it. I can't wait. Just thinking about it – my God! – I've almost spunked my load inside my trousers! Try not to be too promiscuous during the week.

Save all your juice for Friday.

So until Friday at 8.00 pm. I said on the phone that I couldn't promise to behave so, instead, I'll be careful.

       See yer.
        Bye Lover,
         Iain.

PS:– Just to make sure there's no misunderstanding – I'm meeting you outside Lime Street Station, Lord Street entrance, opposite the theatre. OK?

Cheers. xxx'

Booking a room, on the 'phone during my lunch hour (when the office is empty), then, flustered, reading his letter in the lavatory and hoping that the switchboard didn't listen-in when he rang and called me 'baby'.

'I'm sorry I'm late.'

'I thought you weren't coming.'

'I wouldn't have let you down.'

'Then I thought *What if he comes in his leather gear? What'll I do?* I'd have been so embarrassed.'

'No. I brought it in my overnight bag.'

And he closes the hotel door.

'I can't tell you how angry I was with myself when I was driving back up here at the weekend . . . '

Walking around the art gallery and museum with him, looking at Etruscan funerary relics and *The Death of Nelson*.

' . . . It really was a fiasco from Saturday night onwards. Up till then everything was alright as far as I was concerned. You may not have been as experienced as you made out but you more than made up for it when I saw you in the flesh.'

That mean little room with its mean little beds . . .

'I'm sorry it happened so abruptly but I just couldn't have restrained myself any longer. I just had to fuck you.'

. . . with it's weak lights and meagre wallpaper.

'That's the drawback you'll find as you meet other gay guys – primarily they'll want you for your arse. But it wasn't that way with me, honest.'

My hands gripping the bed rail as he pants towards ecstasy, as he sighs into silence.

'One of my great failings is that once I've 'come' I always feel a little depressed with things. And with me feeling the way I usually do, and you being so obviously disgusted with it all – well I just don't know. But please don't think that I just wanted to fuck you then forget about you. I have more feeling than that. and I did enjoy your company . . .'

I need someone.

'. . . although sitting here I'd like to have you with me, let's not get too emotionally involved until we know each other better and longer . . .'

Someone to watch over me.

' . . . And, anyway, when I look back to *my* first experience I remember thinking that *he* was the answer to all my prayers. Until I met someone better looking that is. So don't get carried away with things. Think about it a bit more before you make up your mind about wanting me and I'll do the same. I'm sorry I ended it so bluntly in the car but I'd hate to be hurt again and I'd hate to hurt you.
    Well I'll stop for now.
        Write if you want to.
            Iain.'

Have just phoned your office, Iain, and was told that you are off ill. Are you alright?
Please write or phone soon and put my mind at rest.
I love you.

'Dear R.,
I am writing this to see if I can make amends for that disastrous phone call I made last week. . . .'

Give a guy a break.

'. . . I'm so confused, I'm in a terrible state of depression and your anxious letter made me frantic. I just don't know about anything. I don't want to hurt you, Robbie, that's the last thing I want. I don't want to get more and more attached to you, or you to me, unless I feel that 'this is it.' And that's the problem – I can't be sure. I think I am. Then I think I'm not – God it's been terrible . . .'

Please tell me all the things I want to hear – even if they're not true.

'. . . Things would be different if we were together. But after only a couple of days I don't think either of us can be completely sure about anything. And I couldn't bear the mental strain of being hurt by someone again – or hurting you . . .'

I shall never forget you.

'. . . So please Robbie, understand why I phoned you, and why I'm writing this letter. I'm so mixed up, and so lonely and depressed, I just don't know where I am, or what I feel towards anyone . . .'

You don't have to promise me anything if you don't want to but please write soon – phone sooner. All my love.

'. . . I only hope you are really sure about your feelings for me. As I said on the phone, although I really want you, I also want to be 100% sure it would work and you can't assess that on the strength of one night. So let's just see what happens. When you are apart from someone you are inclined to get an exaggerated perspective on how you feel. It's only after you've been with someone for some time that your true feelings show through . . .'

Yes, I'm sure.
Truly sure.

'. . . please . . . understand. I'm not saying I love you and I'm not saying I don't love you. Christ I just don't know.
    Try to understand.
        I.'

And I'm told to 'take care of myself'.
Then the letters cease.

5' 7"
Blue eyes.
Dark hair.
Slim.

'Sorry mate but I'm looking for someone nearer my own age. Hope you understand.
    Yours,
        Walter.'

37.
No – 35 (sounds better).
Youngish 35.
Darkish hair.
Fairly slim.

'Sorry Pal,
But owing to the large number of replies I am unable to start a scene with you.
    Thanks for writing.
        Keep it clad in leather.
            Micky.'

Eyes – blue.
Height – average.
But now too old to write, or care, or need.
Yet something urges.

'Well, Sir,
Saw your advert in last month's MALEBOX so, – obeying instructions – I am writing.'

'Thanks friend, for your letter but I'm no longer 'available' in the way you'd hoped . . .'

My interests are many and varied.

'. . . – In the meantime I'm returning your photograph. It was very good of you to send it . . .'

I have a sneaking admiration for Carl Orff.

' . . . I do hope that you will eventually find what you're looking for in life.
        God Bless.
         Richard.'

Dear Friend, in reply to a recent chain letter . . .

Wishing to meet.
YoungishmanThirtyfiveFairlyslimDenimfriendsLeathermates21+.
But OH! too old to write, too old to care, too old to need.
I'll close for now.
Look forward to hearing from you.
Yours always.
With no hope, with none at all.

'Peace and Love' from Peter in Australia, who teaches primary school, who plays ('Amongst other things') squash ('Sex topping the list of course!'), whose 13½ stones live in the inner suburbs of Sydney, whose hair is fair and who, when he is able to visit England, would like me to meet his smooth complexion; Clifford and John from South Africa, who write in clear, legible copper-plate script: John, who is thirty six ('But doesn't look it') and Clifford, who loves watching well-built men play football in tight, white shorts, John who likes to grease up his gear with lanolin and to go scuba-diving somewhere in The Transvaal, 'Drop me a line if you can' and 'Yours Faithfully' on lined, beige foolscap; Roger in Belgium telling me how surprised I must be to hear from a lusty 170lb pilot with a bungalow, who can hardly wait to hear from me, signing himself 'Hotlicks – your new-found friend in leather' with a biro on dirty continental writing paper; Jon in Washington who 'does pretty interesting work for the Federal Power Commission,' who is 'proud to be able to work for my country', who advises me to 'take care' of myself and, above all, to 'play it cool'.

All the sad young men.
St John, Billy, Iain.
Love me! Love me! Love me! Say you do.
Bastards.
BASTARDS!
Eileen, Tony, Maisie, John, Kevin, Helen.
O my children, my poor children.
A voice is heard crying aloud.
OH mammy, oh mam.
A threnody for the fallen.

Trees, shrubs, flowers, all hang in the limpid haze with the air like liquid fire. Buildings – burnished in the morning – now blaze under the afternoon sun, the bricks hot to the touch. Bodies naked to the waist. Water. Flesh. Men. The wet bodies of men, their lightly-toasted skin with dark hairs clustering around the heavy nipples, hanging nipples, running into their dark-brown navels. Sheer desire melts, seeps, dissolves into the loins as they pass revealing, half-revealing, touching, half-touching their wonderful breasts, their slightly acrid-smelling crutches, as more heat hangs down, weighted, heavy, everything on fire. Over the skin run secret thrills that dance silently, as more ravishing flesh than you can bear saunters past. As you long to be between someone's legs, taking them into your mouth. Passionate, silent, demonic thoughts – locked away, hidden – dark and hot down below the waistline.

Waiting for nightfall.

Sitting quietly in this quiet room high above Corporation Liverpool. Their fingers drumming silently in the silent flat. And the folded bed. And the smell of age. Cheap cut-glass – white and orange – along the cluttered sideboard, the very moquette faded to the touch. And the gathering dark. With noting to say.

They are thirteen floors up, high above the main road, watching Liverpool stretch far away towards the horizon – smoky.

'Lovely sky,' he says.

'Yer,' Says his mother whose frail fingers rub her forehead then run through hair yellow with age – tangled. Eighty years. God what a time!

Intermittently they talk of relations long dead or not seen since the last Labour victory, or who live, forgotten, outside Cork.

So still, no noise. Motionless in the darkened, darkening room. No movement except for the green display dial of the digital clock ticking silently from the seconds, to the minutes, to the hours – 17.50, 17.53, 17.55 – and the Sunday news, in colour, at the farther end of the room.

Remembered Thursdays – going to the swimming baths – two by two in long rows from school, wearing those rough blue cotton swimming trunks with inadequate elastic – perished from the chlorine.

The news finished – switched off.

'Short and sweet,' she says chirpy in the aching dark. Then the noisy hum of the invisible central heating, and back to the crushing silence between sandwiches.

Time passes, time passes. Tick – tock. The pulsating green dot marking the seconds. Tick. Tock. What do we do with life? How do you fill in the time? What with?

A Sunday afternoon at home.

Waiting for nightfall.

'Are you open yet pal?'

'This is a gay club.' Scrutinised at the door by a suspicious young man.

'Yes, I know.'

'I haven't seen you here before,' through a small opening in the narrow alley door.

'I came here about two years ago.'

'Who with?'

'A friend.'

And cautiously he lets me in.

Down into the cool cellar to where a dreamboat might be waiting, to where they'll look and fight to speak to you, to where you'll be carried off to an exciting bed and the start of an affair to remember.

Red plush and fading leatherette.

A few men scattered about the two large basement rooms which stretch down towards a dance-floor – deserted and unlit.

And the concealed, illicit lighting.

And in your half-lit mind's eye huge physiques sweating into lust.

(Stop thinking with your prick for God's sake!)

'Ooh she's camp.'

As I walk to the bar.

'Who's she?'

As I get my drink and next to me a gorgeous bearded number who's as sexy as hell.

'Another drink, Love?'

'No – after three of the these I go beserk.'

As I leave the bar, trying to find somewhere to hide.

'They say love is blind – but in her case it's got a bag over its head.' 'But they do say that she's got the most e-nor-mous cock.'

'Mm, nice.'

Couples drift in. Hiding near the juke-box with my drink, afraid of being seen. Spiteful laughter and chit-chat at the bar.

'You lied to me Bobby – your Trev's not running to fat at all. In fact he's quite goodlooking – in this light.'

And Bobby's friend pouts away in gin.

As Bobby's sponge-like hands flap and his grey face twists into a smirk. 'What'll you have? The bromides are on me,' and anxiously looks about as his friend sits stiffly in the booth next to mine, giving himself crowsfeet.

And the amyl-nitrate smelling like rancid diarrhoea. And soft and dark voices from the booth on my right.

'I'm not ashamed of my gayness.'

'*Gayness* – God you make it sound like a small seaside resort on the south coast!'

Grunting into laughter.

'Look at that arse at the bar!'

'Ooh don't – me nerves!'

More men and more men sidle into the club and the bar is glutted with jeans. Ice melting in the drinks, faint stirrings in the heart.

'Look at his fucking legs.'

We croon, we croon.

'Give me two minutes with you, baby.'

'Tell that to the marines.'

'I should be so lucky.'

'I went to his place once. He's a leather freak. Sits around in just boots and a leather jock-strap – dead kinky. And his playroom! Christ Almighty! It's like something out of the Tower of London.'

'God this heat! it's too hot even to wank.'

'What did she give you for your birthday – Chanel? Paco Rabanne?'

'Braggi.'

'She's slipping.'

The club is full now and the noise and the heat and the bodies and the terrible yearnings of the soul.

The haunted look, the trailing fingers, the hand held, half-held, the faint smell of rotten, raw meat. The receding hairline, the drifting, drifting fingers – hanging onto your boy in case someone spirits him away with a well-filled shirt, a big crutch or a handsome bored face, smiling in the dark, predatory on the edges of the dancefloor, peering through the turquoise light at the blue-skinned men with shirts the colour of rainclouds, standing, seeming indifferent to the waiting boys wiggling their bums, aggressive, cocksure – they roam in packs around the edges of the dance-floor – preying and neurotic, cursing the perpetual erection and the warm, seductive lust.

He comes towards my table and something within me quivers (like dry ice) then makes me fume as he looks me over and has the gall to smile. Wanting him to talk me into his bed, yet hating this meat-rack. Cold, silent grins all round as I wait for the inevitable proposition.

The arrival of The Queen of Sheba.

'Glasgow

Dear Robbie,

I hope that you're not annoyed at hearing from me after this length of time, but the fact was that last week I passed through Liverpool on the way back here and much as I wanted to visit you there and then, I thought it would be best to contact you by letter in case your reactions were hostile.

I sincerely hope that they're not. We used to be such good friends, Robbie, and although several years have passed since that hotel fiasco, I would still like to have you. We do, or at least we used to, have other 'material' things in common, too.

I shan't say more at the moment as I don't even know if you're still at the same address. But I would like to hear from you again, even if you don't want to get involved after that.

   Yours
    Iain xxx.'

Well, well – so Iain is still keen.

'Wednesday

Dearest Robbie,

Words, quite honestly, cannot express the joy and excitement of last night when you phoned. I really had given you up. However there must be a God after all, listening to my prayers. I just had to write this small letter tonight as I shouldn't have been able to contain myself otherwise.

I'm really glad too, that things are a bit easier for you, Robbie. I realise you must have been very distraught when I broke it off – rather mercilessly when I look back – what with your mother being unwell, and the problems of your work etc., it must have been a bad blow. Believe me, I went through hell too. I didn't do it lightly. However, as you said, that's all water under the proverbial bridge now.

Don't think this is a lot of 'patter' because it's not – I've really thought of you almost every day since. And especially these last few weeks and last week (when I wrote to you) I hoped and prayed you'd reply. Maybe you and I are telepathic? And don't keep thinking you deceived me – granted you may have done so far as your experience was concerned – but the rest I'm sure would have come naturally to you had you been given the chance. I take it you still fancy leather – I hope so anyway.

And, as I said, I honestly still think the same of you now as I did then – and that's more than I think of anyone else in the world. Believe me, Robbie, I'd give anything for you to be up here. However, for the moment anyway, it can't be. But remember you have me ALWAYS – and I mean that.

So I'd better stop now and do some work. Write soon, if you haven't already done so. I'll write another letter when I get yours.

      All my love,
        Iain. xxxx

PS: I still wear the shirt you sent me that Xmas!'

From now on I won't write anything that will excite him, from now on I'll just try to sway him with words.

                      'Friday June 4th

Dear R.,

Thanks for your letter. I must admit I've been waiting for it to arrive all week.

I told you in my last letter that the way I felt for you hadn't changed, well that's true Rob. I don't think I will ever change towards you, only I wish we could have some time together. It really is bloody awful when you're so far away. But I'm still so in love with you, baby.

I wish you'd put that hotel incident out of your mind FOREVER. Thinking back on it doesn't do any good. Apart from the last night, I really did enjoy it and I think you did too. And don't feel ashamed of the 'leather' bit – there's nothing to be ashamed of. The real problem was that you were just not relaxed – you'd been building up a mental picture before I arrived of what it would be like and when we met, well . . . But make no mistake about it – I fancied you then and I fancy you now. Obviously if I didn't care all that much for you I'd hardly have been so enthusiastic when you phoned last week. I know and appreciate the fact that you were prepared to drop everything and come up here. But that wouldn't have been fair on you. And just because I don't want to drop everything for you makes no difference to the way I feel.

What you must realise with me is that I have had a number of affairs already, and also a corresponding number of heartaches. The next one for me will be IT. The next time will be the one for the rest of my life – YOU I hope. But you are a long way away and had you come up, and then found out we were not made for each other, as the saying goes, then you would have been a damn sight more upset than you were. Knowing each other for a couple of nights is not really enough to drop everything for someone. I've been through it before, and I just couldn't take a chance with you.

As I said before, in a letter I think, I only hope you REALLY know what you feel for me. I hope that the fact that I'm really the first one you've had any real relationship with isn't influencing you and distorting your true feelings. I don't think it is, but I only hope to God I'm right. So give it some hard thought, baby, will you?

I'll try to give you a ring before/during/after the weekend. But write again soon – and long. I really love getting letters from you.

        Take care of yourself, Lover.
        All my love,
           Iain. xxx.'

I wasn't lonely any more and it was good to feel cared for.

'Thanks for the letter. You seem awful down in the dumps, so try to buck yourself up a bit – it mightn't be long now, especially if you could get a job up here through one of the bureaus. You said something about not being able to leave your present job until the end of August, didn't you?

And don't be put off by my telling you of my 'friend' – Alex. I have known him for a long time, so obviously we feel a lot for each other. He's not in love with me or anything. But since I don't have you up here to keep me occupied maybe it's just as well I have him as it keeps me from trawling the cottages in search of a substitute for you . . . '

The dark man.

' . . but stop thinking that I'm likely to say 'Bye-bye bright eyes' – I could never do that to anyone for whom I felt a lot. Even if things don't work out as you and I hope they will, at least you will have me for a life-long friend, if you want. And that wasn't a prelude to saying goodbye either. Somehow you never seem to believe that I am going through exactly what you are. But, I suppose, through experience you will learn to let things take their course no matter what.
So buck up baby,
I.'

Then thinking about an idea, a suggestion . . . Amsterdam . . . 20 guineas . . . Flying from Prestwick daily.

'How are you keeping then? What did the doctor say? If you went, that is. And I suppose you didn't. You'd better watch your health if you're going to feel unwell a lot. I don't want to be going round with an invalid, you know!!

As for me, well, I'm fine but I've had a lot of trouble with the car recently. But gradually I'm clearing off my bills so, you never know, I just might manage to come down there for my holidays. But don't build your hopes up, just in case. Anyway you just might be staying up here by that time, with a bit of luck that might be put right come Sept.

I'm missing you though. Just to see you in the flesh would be great. I don't suppose you could scrape up enough to come to Glasgow for a few days could you? Have you got any idea how much it costs? . . .'

Come to Amsterdam with me and make love under a foreign sky – that way it'll seem a little less sinful.

'. . . if you could, I'm quite sure you could stay with me. I could always tell my father a cock-and-bull story, so long as you gave me warning. So think about it and let me know . . .'

I hope I please you in Holland – yes that will be a good ploy.

'. . . I'm afraid I can't give you a definite time when I can phone you this week. But I'll give you a ring sometime soon. Look after yourself baby.'

Let me know soon (re Amsterdam). You can phone me at the office. But for God's sake keep it clean – walls have ears and so do telephonists (and they have been know to listen.) If they catch you calling me 'darling' they'll burn me and take my P45 away.

'I'll say I fancy going to Amsterdam! But can we afford it? Is it really that cheap? I do have a contact in the BEA. booking office up here, so I'll get in touch with him and let you know all the details and, if the prices are the same as you quoted, we'll book it through the branch up here. Is the last two weeks in August OK?

Well, love juice, I'll probably ring you at the office on Monday, so be good until then. And don't worry yourself sick.

> Love,
>
> xxx.'

Kid the enemy.

> 'Wednesday July 14th
>
> I got your cheque alright – must be great to be rich – and am waiting confirmation of the booking and flight details etc. You've no idea how much I'm looking forward to it. I never really go away to any place on holiday. I usually just potter about in the car but, well, for you baby . . .
>
> It really should be great – just we two together for 7 whole days (not forgetting 8 whole nights!!)
>
> Incidentally how are the power cuts affecting you? I hope you're behaving yourself during the hours of darkness. Up here I'm living the life of a Jesuit – untouched by human hand (my own doesn't count.) I couldn't misbehave even if I wanted to – father has a night-light.
>
> Please ring if you can. I'll write or ring very soon. Drop me a line – it seems weeks since I last had a letter from you.
>
> All my love.
> Kiss. Kiss.'

Yer. Sure.

> 'Monday night.
>
> My Darling Rob,
>
> I hope you don't mind me writing twice within a couple of days but it's just the way I feel. I don't remember having felt for anyone the way I do for you. I really am in love with you, Robbie. You mean everything to me.

That's the reason I'm writing – to cheer *me* up. I'm a bit depressed at the moment, with my cold, and not being able to see or touch you makes me feel worse. My phone call to you today made me feel a lot better. But not hearing from you since last week didn't help matters. I don't want to sound selfish – I realise you have other things to do – but I do so look forward to a letter from you.

I don't know if you'll get this letter before the end of the week – with the post being the way it is – but I'm just living for 11pm on Friday so I can talk with you again.

Well you must have realised by now that I'm pretty stuck on you, to say the least. It's not everyone I'd phone 250 miles for. In fact it's probably just as well you're not on the phone, otherwise I'd have an open line to you all day!! (And don't think I wouldn't !!)

Well not long to Amsterdam now eh? I'm really looking forward to it. I'm getting all my sexiest clothes ready – shirts, jeans etc. I think I told you I've got a thing about slim-line shirts and skin-tight jeans with no underpants on underneath them.

It really is great to find someone like you though. We're so lucky to have found each other and now I can't bear the thought of losing you. I've had affairs with other boys, I must admit, but I've never felt so much for any of them as I do for you. As I've said, the sooner we can get together in a permanent flat the better, eh?

    Well, darling, I must get my beauty sleep.
    So look after yourself.
       All my love,
       Iain XXX.'

'Can you hurry up with that phone pal – it's freezing me bollocks off out here!'

'Saturday

'It was a pity that some swine came to the phone box last night as there was so much I wanted to say.

I can't wait till the next time we meet. I want you so much it isn't true. To hold you, undress you, fuck you – everything. It's really going to be unbearable without you. It'll be alright next time. I think you were a bit disgusted last time but now you know better. Sex is so intimate Robbie – just between the two of us. It makes me feel on top of the world when I think that after we'd had sex there was some of me left inside you and during sex there was part of me in you, too. I just can't tell you how much it means to me – everything. And to know that I'm the only one who has fucked you. It's marvellous to think that you've been mine from the start. I'd love to look after you forever – if you'd want me to. My God – I'm getting sentimental now.

And don't buy any more clothes – you'll make me jealous – but get as much leather gear as you want!

I am looking forward so much to gay Amsterdam, but most of all to YOU.

       Lots of love,
        Iain xxx.'

PS. Oh the most important thing of all and I've forgotten!! We're meeting at Prestwick Airport Hotel on Sunday at about 7 pm. OK?'

He'll be leaving for Prestwick now.
(I didn't pack).
He'll be driving towards the airport thinking of sex.
(I didn't book a train ticket).
He'll be getting an erection.
(The weather report for Scotland is 'fair').
He'll have told Alex some story or other.
(I tingle with dread and excitement).

He'll have driven through the early evening dusk (eyeing the arses of the young men, who, wet-thighed, waded through the purple heather.)

(I agree with my mother, it's a pity my holiday fell through).

He's arriving at Prestwick, he's parking his car, he's booking-in and smiling to the desk clerk.

7pm. 8pm. 9pm. And I go up to my room alone.

The flight is at 10.30 pm.

(The green telephone rings and his familiar voice wheedles through the mouthpiece, 'I have a friend I go to bed with,' from months ago still burns inside me.)

Sitting in the airport hotel bedroom, eating smoked salmon sandwiches, smoking Players No. 6, waiting for me to turn up.

(Telling me in the phone booth, 'Alex says he's in love with me but don't worry, Rob'.)

So long, sucker.

On your way, pal.

He waits. I wait.

In our separate rooms hundreds of miles apart.

And I never see Amsterdam.

A shock of black hair above an insipid face – my new boss – small-minded to the point of invisibility. All day, every day he gives a catalogue of the jobs he has done, is about to do, is going to do, and jobs he might never be asked to do.

Surely this will change?

Yet he'll be there longer than you, will smile fitfully, will sign your early-retirement-through-ill-health card and will make the presentation of the *Teasmade* in a semi-circle of embarrassment, stiff in the boardroom, as the sherry is handed around.

All day, every day he chants a litany of my mistakes – mistakes in addition – 'Oh Christ, you're not one of these people who transposes figures are you?', and payslips not torn off properly, and incorrectly sorted piles bound with elastic bands.

Surely this *must* alter?

'How many jobs have you had anyway?'

Taken by surprise, 'Oh – about four.'

'You make it sound like 104!'

But I haven't had that many. I haven't. And always the gentle women gliding past in blue or beige or multicoloured blouses, their hair falling and their shy smiles above the coffee cups, writing, typing, signing invoices which, in the correspondence racks, stretch down the entire length of one wall – invoices for flags.

The doors leading to the quiet factory where they spin the flags of every nation. Flags to go all over the world. To Norway, Saudi Arabia, Egypt, Singapore, Iraq and the blue ensign for Australia and the warm, Polynesian seas south-east of the equator.

Thirty five, thirty nine, forty and running to seed.

All passion spent.

Settling down under the warm, fluorescent lighting with the soft, brown carpet (in replaceable squares) with the clicking, chattering typewriters.

Then coffee at ten, with the humming telephones. We have all been here for so long – men who have centuries of service and the long-serving women and a man who *actually* lost his arm at Tobruk when he was young and in the desert.

The still, small crying voice in the wilderness.

The order, the routine of things – which once had seemed so secure because it was so unchanging – now frightened him. For it seemed imprisoning this fixed procession of things to be done, duties to be performed, a fixed pattern, a rigid protocol from which there was no escape. It had a volition, a momentum all of its own, and he was merely 'incidental' to it. When he wasn't there it continued, when he was there it sucked him in and subdued him.

Up at seven, Out by eight, Lunch at twelve, Tea at three, Finish at five, Home by six, Bed by twelve.

Mother tenacious over the cooker, worrying about the strict order of meals, the electricity bill and the gas meter, the curtains, the skirting boards, Christmas, birthdays and the price of salmon. Ageing in the afternoon sun, with her varicose veins clustered in her white, painful legs, looking older with her teeth out as she collects her purse, winds the clock and, taking it upstairs to bed with her says, 'Goodnight lad, see you in the morning' and waddling out of sight humming some old, old tune she once heard her father sing.

'God bless mam.'

Then up the stairs to fitful rest with her indefinable fears about her son, suspicious and watchful in bed, in the whispering dark, listening to him sneak out of the flat late at night then back in again, her instinctive dread of something which can't be put into words or smothered beneath a prayer when lighting a candle at a shrine.

And him with his hidden watchful life – spiteful and touchy – wanting her to find a clue or a hint, dreading yet wanting her to see that his secretive undercover could be lifted, be broken so that he could breathe again after ages of suffocation and, after the first terrible, shameful, shaming blush – relief – blessed, blessed relief. Wanting her to know yet taking infinite care she should not find out, suppressing everything, anything which might confirm her doubts.

Longing for grace, for absolution. Yearning for hope.

Hope?

Dread.

Crumbs over everything. Cutlery, crockery not washed properly. General untidiness. Arguments, clashes with her over TV programmes and he *usually* gets his way and if he

doesn't he sulks and emotionally blackmails her. Yet when she speaks it is gentle.
'Can I have the light on, lad?' in that curious, wheedling way of hers, which touches the heart yet makes the blood *boil*.
Of course you can! You don't have to *ask*!

Yet he only nods in the stone-faced silence and guiltily she puts the light on then droops behind the paper and squints down, along the births, deaths and marriages columns or at what her stars say.

Reading in the gathering dark on Sunday afternoons straining her already strained eyes, her blue spectacles rocking on the coffee table, thinking 'He likes the dark, our Robbie.' But it's difficult to see the print. The arguments. The silence. This English boredom. Then his retreat into tears as Mahler revolves at 33 r.p.m. under the anguished window sill.

> *There is an evil under the sun, and it*
> *is common among men.*

There is a vision which comes with growing frequency, one that stands out against all the others – stark and unlovely – the death of the soul. Then gradual hate.

Every Wednesday she goes to the O.A.P club. Every Sunday – rain or shine – down to the Pier Head they go to watch the ships throb out to sea. On Saturday too, if the weather's fine.

And on one Sunday when the weather's crisp, he'll realise he's been doing this for over ten years now, watching the birds flap and cry high overhead, watching the dark water lap and rave, watching the empty city and craving to be far away, beyond the horizon.

He will realise that he is dying the slowest of all deaths. Then he will surrender in the falling, fading half-light and he will say 'Yes, this is what I must accept because this is all there is.' Mother will prod him into conversation when a familiar face is seen, will talk over him, answer questions for him then fall asleep by the sea or on the sofa or call for her cocoa at nine o'clock in bed. There will be the long days and the empty evenings by the hearth, the hidden lechery and the lust for men, the ageing head, the spreading waistline, the calling in the night and the lonely, terrible burning in the loins that must be smothered. Occasionally on some evening, some very late night when his lust cries out, swells up and washes over him, he will sneak into his tight leather clothes and, lurking down alleys, in known toilets, someone will suck away his greed, or a lonely, white young man will slip his penis into his mouth and, kneeling in front of him, carressing his buttocks, he won't feel so alone or aged anymore. Then after it's over the bitter, shameful trek home, creeping into the house so he won't wake her, changing then hiding his clothes. Then, respectable in pyjamas, he makes the cocoa with a clatter and puts it on her bedside table as she wakes, snorting with a start, and pulls the bedclothes back up over herself in quick, embarrassed modesty, with a forced grin and 'Thanks lad,' to his automatic response 'Good night, mam.' Occasionally he will rebel, threaten to leave, even make plans to go back to London (where all the provincial queers go in order to become superb) but his heart won't really be in it. Occasionally he will see adverts which will excite him, make him burst with new hope, but the adverts go unanswered and gradually he will age – he and his mother. Gradually they will grow old together.

Old.

Old.

And the sea.

His decline was not sudden or dramatic but imperceptibly gradual.

Slowly – very slowly – he went downhill.

Middle aged, forty, fifty.

Even his passions had become commonplace.

And mother creeping beyond eighty.

Moving through the hospital looking at the words which have the power to terrify – 'Physiotheraphy', 'Pathology', 'Intensive Care' – we stand, my brothers and I, outside the ward coughing loudly, then smiling as other families drift in huddles at the doors, bringing chocolates and fruit for their cherished sick.

The closed doors of radiography.

Nurses competent with death, quadrille down the tiled corridors, glancing at watches, late for duty.

We all whisper – as if at school – the talking subdued and initmate . . . cars, babies, exams, 'Our John's doing well', 'Pat likes her job but she's becoming a bit of a handful', smiles, puns, jokes with vast, obscene subtexts – and the flowered screen quivering around her bed . . . Oh mam . . . as suddenly we burst in upon the sacred quiet of the Sunday ward, and the laughing of the eyes, and the hands raised and clasped and 'Will she be alright? Will she be alright?' as she sits in the bed as cuddlesome, as rosy as a doll, but the back arching a little more, the hair thinning out, the scalp as pink and thin as eggshell. And her tired, ancient heart.

Then for the first time in all these years, I realise that she is mortal.

And slowly, imperceptibly, they began to grow like each other. And slowly, imperceptibly, a silence grew between them which they knew only death could end. And slowly, imperceptibly, they began to long for it, to wish for it and – in their most secret dreams – to plan for it.

And at last it came.

On a saturated Wednesday afternoon when the rain ceased and a driving drizzle blew up, which chilled even the bones. And the naked, wet trees shivering in small, black groups.

His thin, weak voice (all teeth and adenoids) comes

wheedling over her small, humble coffin, towards the pews.

I am from God and unto God I will return

My hair won't part properly, it's all on one side.

Oh Lord have mercy upon this poor sinner

The flowers in their silver bowls, the elegant candles, The Stations of the Cross with Helen. And, perfect in death, a halo of saints smile down from the roof.

'I was awfully sorry to hear about your mam, Robbie' – near the bus stop.

An arm touched, a shoulder rounded.

'Please accept our condolences', inside the grief-filled lift where her body stood, upright, on its pine-and-silver end. The remnants of the family huddled before the altar rails, wailing and calling but nothing could ease or soothe.

O Pain, O Death

'She was smashin', your mam.'

And George, ('When you die Nell, I'll be the miserablest son-in-law in the world'), crying. 'I won't 'alf miss Nellie.'

O my sisters weep.

The priest signals and she is lifted shoulder-high. Then we carry her home.

Not this! Not this!

One needs something cold and diamond-hard.

At last it has come.

The journey to the grave.

And the house is so *cold* and the silence broken only by the sobs of the girls and the lads look grim and red-eyed and both sets of in-laws look uncomfortable, embarrassed by all this passionate English grief. Is it possible that she is gone? Is it possible?

The echoing church, the grey stone, the polished pews, the empty altar, the Victorian stained glass of the Sacred Heart then the priest and white surplice, and the dismissal to the earth and we – her boys – carry her to her God.

Is it possible to be so broken?

Is it possible that she is *gone*?

Is it . . . *possible*?

And all the times we ever argued come back to me, and *worst of all*, the many stinging things I said to her leap up and shout my treachery, everything that was vile in my life rises up in front of me to mock and taunt and ulcertate my grief!

The lynch-pin of our lives is gone.

With a quick ceremony, with a little pomp we leave her in the earth.

The cars glide home.

Life hangs in the distance like a tolling bell.

And home isn't home anymore.

The withered edges of the cemetery, the solemn neatness and arriving back alone to the house.

The car doors bang then glide away.

A death in the family bringing the death of the family.

The girls will sit broken and lacerated in chairs, the lads will go to bed early and weep into the bed clothes, their children will not play near the house, meals will be eaten in grief-stricken silence – for a while, for a while.

But I shall keep my vigil, I shall cherish my grief, I won't forget – oh mummy *I'll* never forget as I sit here in the damp and weep and weep.

Then going through her clothes, her treasured belongings was the most terrible, the most agonising thing of all. And there is *so* little that was hers – clothes made for her, clothes she'd been given, her large collection of cheap shoes, her small watch, her large, unsightly underwear, her handkerchieves, the chest of drawers filled with dun-coloured nylons, her religious relics, her photos, her teeth and her vulgar bric-a-brac.

And oh the quiet!

And oh mummy I want you!

I'm too old to enjoy my freedom. I don't want to be *alone*! I'm looking for someone to change my life. I'm looking for a miracle in my life.

And slowly, imperceptibly, he feels the full horror of his dreams – and he can only cry out, he can only howl out his misery and his raw, fresh terror – M A M ! over and over again.

Next day it snowed. There were knocks on the door – frequent and anxious – but he couldn't bring himself to answer. Slowly the dust settled around the house and days passed in a sort of numbing paroxysm of grief.

Then after many days hunger forced him out, with the green striped shopping bag, and outside the snowflakes drifted down and hunger and cold gnawed away at him – diminishing his grief, if only a little.

But the break from the house merely sharpened his sense of loss, and the house seemed *so, so* empty when he got back, so stale to the smell and, feeling as though he'd betrayed her, he wept into his soup.

It snowed for many days, with the temperature dropping, until even sitting with his overcoat on wasn't warm enough. So he lit the fire. And every action which ensured his survival seemed profane, seemed a denial of his grief.

And slowly he began to eat regularly, to shave, to clean, to rake the ashes from the grate, until finally, he returned to work.

But his grief throbbed inside him like a small altar flame which he kept alive, which brought tears at meal times or at Christmas or on those rare occasions when he spoke to her and heard her laughter echoing through the house.

The handfuls of earth, the rain, the Sunday visits to her grave with flowers.

All day it has rained. Gales driving in from the Atlantic, from the St George's Straits way across from Ireland. The river is lost in grey drizzle. Scattered blocks of flats stand – naked and thrashed – in the failing grey light and the town is lashed into winter and the windows bend.

Behind the panes, along a pink-flowered window seat, toys are scattered – an upright doll, a red and yellow fire engine, a small clown, bright red wood blocks. Across the white, warm hearth rug a magic colouring book, a saucer of water, a paint brush, some crayons – the crumbs of cake. A sleepy, sleeping, pink and white, milky boy sighing in warm luxurious syrup. Even the fire spits quietly except for an occasional crackle and then the boy's eyes half-open, his fingers half-clench into a fist then relax again as he slips back into the warmth of sleep. The glowing wood, the sheen of paper, brass ashtrays glinting in the late afternoon half-light, the shining walls, as this boy sleeps after having played alone all afternoon, all day – long, long ago.

All day it has rained. And the house is quiet as the wind howls and curses, driving rain into cracks under wood, behind soaking bricks and plants shake and drench, eaves drip, leaves shiver, cats curl and blink through glass then sidle up to the fire, stretch and claw on the hearth rug then purr into a snooze.

This delicious, voluptuous ambiguity. Shaking curtains, the rattle of windows, the steady howl of the wind, the rain cascades over this northern, this collier town in grey January – long, long ago.

> *On a mountain stands a lady,*
> *Who she is I do not know,*
> *All she wants is gold and silver,*

All she wants is a nice young man.
So call in your very best friend

A *nice* young man,

your very best friend

A nice *young* body,

your very best friend

A nice young *cock*.

So call in your very best friend,
While I go out to play-ay-ay-ay.
On a mountain stands a lady . . .

Children calling in the streets, the shepherdess calling to the shepherd as summer dies, the thud of a boat, rippling water dappled and shady, shoes shaped like coffins, and coal dust on the grass on a sunny, windy afternoon with sandwiches.

The desire for flesh, the old, the eternal ache. And the failing grey light. And the mythical length of the penis – nine glorious inches! Inglorious lust.

Buying apples – green and peppery – in the deserted, early, damp evening.

Heartlessness.

Golden wheat in England. Decline and Fall. Calling on the wind.

And the lurking libido.

Running my hands over the firm white flesh of his smooth buttocks. 'Oh you've got a fucking gorgeous arse!' pushing my penis between his soft, hard thighs and shooting between his wonderful, muscular legs.

> *In the morning sow thy seed, and in the*
> *evening withold not thine hand.*

And this man spread eagled against the wall, whose name is Alan or Chris or Keith, who breathes 'Get down on it!' over and over again as I unbutton his shirt and wildy devour his chest, sucking the heavy nipples – biting into them sharp and sudden – licking my way down to his navel, to the ultimate joy.

Kneeling in front of him, his clothes open, he is naked and raw and massive. 'Get down on it! Oh, for Christ's sake, get it into your mouth!' in quiet, uneasy ecstasy. Greedily, hungrily, he rams it home.

And on his right forearm a tattooed sword encircled by the name 'Debbie'. A few sad minutes. I only met him this evening. I look silly kneeling here in skin-tight leather at my age.

'I'm coming! Oh Jesus Christ I'm coming!'

His sperm is sweet to the taste. He is warm yet hard. Swallowing his very essence.

The lower depths.

All day it has rained.

Slipping gently, gently away into the gentle coma of late middle age. All day it has rained.

All, all day.

> *But know thou that for all these things*
> *God will bring thee into judgement.*
> *For God shall bring every work into*
> *Judgement, with every secret thing, whether*
> *It be good, or whether it be evil.*

It all starts here – the collecting and the closet-lust.

> *Therefore put away evil from thy flesh*

It all starts *here* with the air turning warm for Spring, with the sun filtering through the naked, empty trees yet hope in the heart and the yellow morning light. It all begins here, now, on the edges of the park, with the overcoat open, the loosened scarf, the morning tea, the delicate hands, the small, balletic birds and magazines full of more exquisite young men than you will ever see. Hidden in drawers, to be unlocked, to be lingered-over in the private dark.

*And further, by these,
my son be admonished.*

It all starts – here – with the pain curling around the left shoulder blade, then throbbing its way down to the heart, so that you've got to sit down on the bench, below the twittering, invisible birds. School girls with satchels giggling towards school and shoppers looking prim as they trek towards town on this April morning. As the pain knots below the ribcage then unravels itself away leaving your left side tingling, warm with fear.

The judgement and the mercy of God.

The dizziness, the reeling, the falling down. It all happens here, on your sixtieth birthday, in the park, in Spring.
This is how it was.
This is how it will always be.
Time.
Time.
Gradually I've got used to it. Gradually I've begun to like it – the solitary flat and the silent rooms. Gradually it has enveloped me until now I feel quite secure, womb-like. When one of my brothers or sisters visit (which is rare now) I appear happy to them, benign to my grown nieces and nephews and even grand nieces.

And, you know, it's strange how little in common I have with them. My family, their children, their children's children, seem perfect strangers to me, remote or embarrassed when they're here, pulling faces when forced to come. Sometimes there's a wedding or an engagement or a death or a christening and I have to go and drink among so many people I don't know, people who look at you with sharp eyes, people who frighten me. I always leave early pleading age.

And gradually I don't want them to visit me anymore – occasionally I don't answer when they knock.

Gradually one stops seeing them. Gradually one is weaned away from them too, and years literally, *years*, go by without us even meeting – my brothers, my sisters and me.

And the days come and go. Falling, inch by inch, into a slow decline, a gradual decay. Not caring. Not wanting to. As, one by one, the family succumbs to internal diseases contracted long ago, or silent cancer noiselessly consuming the bowels, or ulcers perforated in the duodenum, or heart attacks behind closed doors.

One by one the family creeps silently away.

And gradually they've become memories, phantoms – like Arcadia – and all our pain and joy seems trivial now, now that mum is no longer here to bind us together into a family. Because my brothers and sisters were parents in their own right and have strangers to mourn them which seems so very curious to me the youngest of the brood.

Yet even though he'd been the youngest of seven there were disturbing signs.

Just lately, my left side – from the shoulder to the kneecap – has begun to tingle, permanent pins and needles. Just lately I've felt dizzy. On the stairs, in the kitchen, even lying down. Just lately I've begun to swoon and fall.

Sometimes it's difficult to know whether or not there is any feeling in the fingers of my left hand. Sometimes my eyes ache and rattle in my head for hours on end. I lie down quite often now – too often perhaps, after work, during the day, on Sunday afternoons with the papers strewn about the sofa and the tea things scattered over the mat.

Just lately I've begun to get frightened.

Just lately I've needed mummy a lot.

More and more the dull throb in my chest, more and more the fire in the temples rages.

Then quite suddenly he was aware of the fatality of illness.

Quite suddenly he was aware that life had gone by.

Quite suddenly he was aware that he had become *old*.

> *There is no remembrance of former things;*
> *neither shall there be any remembrance of*
> *things that are to come with those that*
> *shall come after.*

He could see – in all its stark eloquence – one vision fading as a new one arose. At first it was a mere suggestion, not even a half-thought, yet gradually it recurred until it was concrete. Then it became fixed. And, once fixed, it had only to be fulfilled.

The image was of a man on the verge of decrepitude.

There he sat with his round spectacles, his white hat, his straggling hair, mopping his forehead, wiping his small mouth, looking about him at the historic buildings, with no interest or enthusiasm.

Just filling in time.

A lonely old man, on holiday abroad, joylessly seeing the world.

There were other visions – fragmentary and horrifying – the viscid pool with the tubular batons of human shit floating into the mouth as you fell in, stinking and fetid. The vast cathedral with the steps and the unseen pursuers in the night, in the night, in bed – alone and afraid of the dark.

The family gone. The friends lost. The heart not in things anymore.

Once I had so much hope.

Once I could have been a king among men.

Once.

But now? The fixed vision. The death wish.

> *The thing that hath been, it is that which shall be:*
> *and that which is done is that which shall be done; and*
> *there is no new thing under the sun.*

He will become like all old men – be irritable with children, short-tempered with loud street games, anxious about the delivery of the papers, eagle-eyed at the window if there's a sudden noise outside. He will become a vain, a slightly pathetic old man on holiday in Rome, reading *The Four Quartets*, hoping that someone will notice and be impressed. Daily looking at his static grey hairline, waiting for the yearned-for 'You certainly don't look your age,' from sympathetic ladies (from the Home Counties) on the coach.

'Well, I'll be in my sixties soon,' he says with an old smile, with a practised modesty, then throws his light beige raincoat around his shoulders just like an actor did in a film once.

Sitting at the café table, watching the young men sauntering by, or near the river, their burnished skins glowing in the evening sunlight – oh yes! – Godlike as they chuckle or smile or try to cadge a cigarette or a sandwich from your packed lunch and *oh yes!* their *marvellous* teeth and firm bodies. And ample women in black, something eternal in the air, the timelessness of the ancient, the *very old*. Picking our way around St John Lateran or Mary Major with the quiet nuns. Roofs of beaten gold, and twisted turquoise columns in *Romanesque* from the guide book.

'Adistra' meaning right.
'Sinistra' meaning left.
And always on my holidays, alone, in August.

> *Rejoice, O young man, in thy youth; and let*
> *thy heart cheer thee in the days of thy youth,*
> *and walk in the ways of thine heart,*
> *and in the sight of thine eyes.*

(His nipples showing through his white shirt)

> *The eye is not satisfied with seeing,*
> *nor the ear filled with hearing.*

('Oh he's *nice*' – in the Piazza Navonna)

> *Better is the sight of the eyes than*
> *the wandering of the desire.*

And all the time the comic Americans, in coach loads, looking down the Forum towards the Atrium Vestae.
'Well, would you look at that, George!'
George in a pork-pie straw hat waddles to her 200lb side and squints, in shorts, at all this bewildering, ancient rubble.
'Yeah!' he says in a bored, middle-western accent, 'It's all so like – arh, *old*.' Then they both take pictures, waddle back to the coach like two round 'o's and do Europe in a fortnight.
Walking down the Via Sacra from the Colosseum – his Home Counties lady trying to think of an excuse to get away from him and the potted history – 'To the left the Basilica Julia, and down on your right the Senate House where Cicero delivered the Phillipics against Anthony – Caeser bleeding to death in the Theatre of Agrippa – or was it the Marcellus Theatre? The legions, the eagles, Jupitor Stator, the Temples of Mars and the Baths of Diocletian' – with such information

he bored his companions who went with him once (and only *once*) on frigid tours around the city.

*I communed with mine own heart; yea my heart
had great wisdom and knowledge and I gave my heart
to know wisdom, and to know madness and folly.*

(Oh! He is gorgeous!)

He waited, he *lived* for his August escapes, for his yearly enchantment in a Greek courtyard, under the olive trees, in a warm seductive village in Tuscany or Aix-en-Provence. Olive skins and vineyards. And Bacchanalian nights under the hot Italian stars.

(Oh he is gorgeous!)

*For in much wisdom is much grief and he that
increaseth knowledge increaseth sorrow.*

(Christ! I wouldn't mind getting my mouth around him!)

Pain recollected in tranquility, as it shoots into his eyes – cupping his hands in his lap – as he draws in breath quickly through his teeth, as the sharp pain convulses his left side, making his foot curl inwards from the instep to the ankle.

The birds flying into the English park as the wind slices into his skin, and the Italian boys seeming so very far away now, as he walks slowly through the manicured grass, down the gravel path towards the gates.

Home to an empty house.

Home to the grave.

The lock, the brass key, the door banging-to, as afternoon lengthens into evening.

But I feel so dizzy.
I feel so *ill*.

> *And all the rivers run into the sea; yet the sea
> is not full; unto the place whence the rivers come,
> thither they return again.*

I'll lie down on the couch for a while.

> *And the sun goeth down;*

Listen. Can you hear it? The singing? *Listen* – Oh can you *hear* it?

> *My Yiddisher Momma,
> I miss her more than ever now*

Yes, they are all here.

I can summon them up from the empty house, from the shuttered rooms, from the staircase creaking into silence, from the wind blowing around the moon. From the frail, dead dark they come – my family and me – in a stately, courtly, purple cavalacade. Softly, very, very softly all my ghosts begin to chatter and cough, murmuring in the cold, damp dark.

My sisters – their warm, and scented exquisite feminity, their flesh flushed in make-up and their silky hair falling across an eye. Hair as soft as down, misty-eyed and shining-lipped, caught in an embrace, then bending down to kiss me. Their arms, their bodies smelling like paradise, their perfumed kisses showering down on me, pouring delicious sensations into my ear. And scented money pressed into my hands, as their boyfriends whistle and call from the dark rain, in blue drapes, from beyond, from behind the vestibule door.

My brothers naked and brilliantined – in crisp, white

shirts. Working-class gigolos with money to spend, and the hard knot of their bodies – stripped and washed and raw as meat under the hot water and green washing soap. Their legs wide apart, powerful and tensed, their torsos their biceps, pink and taut – swollen masculinity squeezing into underwear.

Yes, all are come.
All are dancing.
In this ghostly, majestic minuet.

> *One generation passeth away, and*
> *another generation cometh;*

So he lies here, in this tomb, listening to the clocks, to the creak of the furniture, to the stairs settling into silence and, like his mother before him, sees the house fill with faces, hears laughter from decades ago, echoing through the house and hears her light, mellifluous voice singing in the dark.

> *Oh I get the blues*
> *When it's ray-ay-ay-nin,*
> *The blues I can't lose,*
> *When it rains.*

Hold me close mam. Take me in your arms when I'm feeling low.

> *It rained when I met you*
> *It rained when I lost you*
> *So I get the blues when it rains.*

We are *young*, WE ARE.
Somewhere between sixty and death.
My friend you are dying.
My friend you are ill.

Wind and the steady, steady heartbeat of the rain whispering against the window glass.

Come hence, do not tarry.

Wraith-like figures leave the walls, calling softly to me. The muffled drum. The cortege.

'Look, Rob, we've got the ring!'

Is that you Maisie? Oh Maisie is that *really* you?

'Come on, Robbie, lad!' From the three lads.

Oh Helen.

Oh Eileen.

Mummy – oh mam – is it possible to love her so much? Is it *possible*?

And her warm, lovely voice filling the whole house, the parlour, the back kitchen, then receding up the stairs, into infinity.

'Come on, lad, up the dancers.'

'Has my cocoa got half-a-crown on it mam?'

'How much do you love me?'

'A pound of sugar!'

'Oh lad, Oh son.'

She fades, dissolves away on a smile, her soft hands waving goodbye at the school gates and her mouth quivering into tears.

And in this small intimate circle (as gentle as a kiss) they hover, around his eyes, around the sofa, then begin – one by one – to drift back into the woodwork.

Eileen, Tony, Maisie.

Kevin, John, Helen.

Mum waving in a brown coat – then gone.

When I sleep will I dream?

How much do you love me?

1, 2, 3, 4, 5. Once I caught a fish alive.

Then the dream-like visions of this brief episode curl and

vanish and all is still, still as glass.
Feeling so bad.
Afternoon gliding into evening.

Contrition it is that getteth forgiveness.

Lie down. Close your eyes and pretend.
Something is coming. He stands on the threshold of something unknown and terrible – the pinnacle of fear – with the left hand side of his body intermittently going numb, tingling back into sensation, as the jaw-line drops. The steady rain kissing the window panes, showering the window sill outside.
And in his mind anything is possible.
In his mind anything can happen, when he closes his eyes he controls destiny, when he closes his eyes he can shut out all those terrible English visions.
The room is long and black now.
His white, blank face staring.
The curtains – merging into high dusky shadows – drape dark to the floor.
Only the window is plain – then the man.
The window is shuttered but a single shaft of sunlight blazes through the many slats of the Venetian blind, casting a rich glow over this man – this ill, ill man – in late spring, in this exquisite, lonely room. Dusty air lazily floating around this small, prostrate figure, with hair like fog. He rises with difficulty, then goes *into* the shaft of slattered sunlight and partially opens the blind. And more light than is imaginable roars into the static, hot room. And his face is blotted out for a moment, then glows like alabaster as the limpid eyes close and his black arms reach through the sun. As he utters a single word – 'Mummy.'
And the finite knocking.
The reeling to the ground.

Leave me in my own house, for God's sake – leave me in peace.

'Come on, Pop, you'll be alright!'

> *Whither art thou going thus gaily?*
> *Hast thou thy maker forgot?*
> *Come hence do not tarry.*

Everything – my whole body – aches and throbs. No spittle.

And all about him the minutiae, all the memories of sixty years of being alive.

Today – gone.

Everything bathed in a yellow evening sunlight and golden, this light after the rain in a slow, genteel, northern death.

The soft hum of the distant traffic.

> *It pleaseth God well.*

Evening falling into night. Heavy clouds gathering in a greying sky with the sun squinting through – like a dully, yellow eye weeping.

> *The time is at hand.*

Death and Transfiguration.

> *And the sun goeth down,*
> *And all the rivers run into the sea;*
> *And yet the sea is not full,*
> *But the earth abideth forever.*

Part Three
THE WALK TO THE PARADISE GARDEN

See, O Lord, and consider.
How is the gold become dim, How
is the most fine gold changed.

I want the sun to warm, to sink into these old, long bones, the years that have *ached* away. *From the candy store on the corner,* pink and white striped canopies rustling in spring sunshine or sharp, arthritic winds biting into crouched overcoats, homburgs shaking under shaking hands, *from the candy store on the corner to the chapel on the hill* – no, that's not it, *two young lovers went there walking* – no, that's not it either . . . rain crashing against reeded windows. I feel a dying away, an ebbing of the spirit, like wine on marble with just a few, *few* traces of where it once was. Steel grey skies, clouds, sweltering heat and dusty pear trees growing out of concrete. An ebbing away, dying is so easy like this at two o'clock, in shadows. Miss Allen, oh Miss Allen, you were my first school teacher all those years ago, I cried and played with cardboard money and was an angel at Christmas . . . yet it's hard to believe, hard to accept that this body, now so acutely decayed, could once have throbbed and been so vibrant. The school bell tinkling over Brae Street on a long summer's day, the caterpillar, an ancient tree, a dry road droning under heat, a Union Jack flapping at the elbows on Empire Day, Coronation mugs, rustling taffeta – those skirts with acres of underskirts. Yet the girls always smelt so pretty, so cool . . . Flood the age-soaked memory with remembrances, glory in the cruel exaltation of the spirit, *from the candy store on the corner to the chapel on the hill*, tell me, oh tell me things I want to hear . . .

'Mother,' He cried out.

But no one heard.

> *How doth the city sit solitary, that*
> *was full of people. The elders have*
> *ceased from the gate, the young men*
> *from their music. The precious sons*
> *of Zion, comparable to riches, how*
> *are they esteemed as earthen pitchers.*

An early morning, a bright day. A day for looking out of windows in a late, windy afternoon. Into the cold kitchen, shaking in the chilly air, making porridge in a pan. On her own, eating porridge for breakfast alone and hands shaking through the meal, with the little finger of the right hand crooked – lady like. Above her old bed *Let not thy heart be troubled* and photographs of her when she was young, with peaches-and-cream skin not wrinkled and stiff and creaking to the floor to say her prayers. Two photos of her and her Tom, him in a soldier's uniform and a side view of her with a headband hanging down, just like Isadora Duncan.

'In the old days we only had an outside lav and no bathroom. You had to wash one leg one week and your other leg the following week.' Well remembered hardships, cherished like battle-scars, for it was these things that made you what you are, and why today's generation have never had it so good, and there isn't no backbone anymore. In her trembling memory she's a girl of nineteen and a flapper of the

'20s. But they didn't *roar*. They were loud, vulgar days but no, they didn't roar, the side kicks of the Charleston seen again after many years, *many* years, winning TV dancing medals but still recognizably the Charleston.

She scratches her old, grey head and smiles. Walking with a tripod is hard though. But it's made of chrome. It shines so. She pats her old, high bed and smiles.

Oh Tom . . . Oh Tom . . .

Finishing her porridge she lets the spoon fall into a sprial around the plate. Finishing her porridge she sits there, lost in antiquity, with her right hand holding the plate and her left hand tapping lightly on the counterpane. And death no longer seeming important, but quite a natural end to all this, death seeming almost civilized and 'Lots of flowers. I do like flowers, those white ones with the long stems . . . ' and the gloss of new wood embedded with silver-gilt handles, the ostentation of a Rolls, the nodding of heads.

But the silence between the meals gets longer, and the effort to move harder, and soon it is difficult for Rosie to walk from one room to another. The place is the first to go. After a lifetime of polishing, she gives in, lets the dust cascade down, showering everything with a fine film, darkening the mirror and the window panes till finally the light takes on a curious, congested, heavy quality, as it falls in angular columns to the floor.

Next the dishes. They are left till they fill the sink, the dresser, the television, the bedroom until, reduced to one cup, one saucer, one plate, one knife, she gradually reduces what she eats till it becomes mere picking from packets. Then the time between meals gets longer, until finally she ceases to eat altogether. Last, it is herself which, once falling, declines quicker than all the rest. Her clothes, once so crimped and starched, are left, until they too form a second skin, not taken off, but left with the colour and smell of her very soul. Finally she takes to her bed, and the days pass in a succession of happy, half-dreams, intermittent knocking then silence, the glass-like quiet remaining unbroken. But the time between sleeping and the knocking gets shorter, until faces appear above the bed, and uniformed hands lift her from the eiderdown. 'Oh it hurts!' and 'Oh leave me in my own home,' and 'Come along dear, you'll be alright,' and 'Oh Tom!' and: Committal!

'Oh Tommy!'

'Tom!' cried out in the ambulance, the home, the ward. But no-one heard.

> *Turn thou us unto thee, O Lord*
> *Renew our days as of old.*

Miss Jordan had taught all her adult life. She had never wanted to do anything but teach. And she had pursued her goal with a Catholic single-mindedness. Her life was her work and her pupils were *her children*. But life had not been kind to Miss Jordan, as she returned every night of every year to her large, Victorian house on the edge of the park.

The school holidays were agony. Some days she never left the house at all, and her mother kept pressing the bell throughout the day and half the night. Slowly she began to drink secretly, self-consciously, in the lounge with her ram-rod back at least six inches away from the back of the chair. Insidiously, the drinking became heavy until, at times, she didn't even hear or answer mother's night bell. 'It's just a small drink,' she'd say to herself, 'Just a tiny one . . . ' To ease the aching loneliness of the holidays, when there were no excercise books to correct, as she tried to listen to Mozart on the radio. Then school would resume and she would see her children again, and the drinking would cease.

'Then suddenly mother died.'

One dreadful night after the funeral, the house was so silent, so empty, so cold, 'And I couldn't face going back to it after school.' So her drinking resumed, even during term time, and eventually whole nights were spent in alcohol, and even if she chewed currants or cachous it still failed to kill the smell on her breath. And then the headmistress found her one day, stumbling around the classroom, falling against the bookshelves, falling to the floor, and the children crying or saying, 'Miss Jordan's sick,' or running into the green corridor outside.

When she left, after they made her resign, it was worse even to go out for the groceries. She had them delivered like the booze.

But the house was so *big*, so cathedral-like. And her ram-road back never once touching the back of the chair, not arching as they ushered her into the ambulance, as she thought, 'Dear God, they're taking me into a home', and the whole house empty, silent . . . and dust settling on the Victorian furniture in every room . . . and the stairs creaking . . . and the vestibule door, with its coloured glass, banging-to.

Miss Jordan received over one hundred letters from her pupils in the first week after her dismissal. The next week she received none. As they placed her in bed she cried out.

But no-one heard.

> *The Lord hath afflicted me in the*
> *days of his fierce anger.*
> *He hath sent fire into my bones.*
> *The Lord hath delivered me into their*
> *hands, from whom I am not able to*
> *rise up; I weep; mine eye, mine eye*
> *runneth down with water, because the*
> *comforter that should relieve*
> *my soul is far from me; my sighs are many*
> *and my heart is faint.*
> *I am desolate and the enemy*
> *have prevailed.*

Like Pop, like Rosie, like Miss Jordan, Annie Gaffney had worked her way through the other wards until she too had arrived at Poplar.

She was the last of a generation of flower sellers – when you wanted flowers for your wedding you went to Annie Gaffney. She'd take your order, she'd laugh and joke, she'd look like Betty Hutton. Then when the great day came, she'd bring the flowers around in a big wicker basket on one of her tremendous arms.

Wherever flowers would sell, Annie would be there – the hospital at visiting time (Sundays especially), the station during the week (on the corner in cold weather), even Yew Tree cemetery. 'Where me mam's buried,' – her mam who taught her how to croon and sell, who taught her how to wrap silver paper around blooms, then arrange them in pink and white waves in the basket and *always* to ask a fair price. 'I miss me mam,' she'd say when her birthday came around, or at Christmas, when she missed her most of all. When they'd both been standing together in Lime Street shouting and offering carnations to passing trade, and then, with swollen fingers, slipping into *The Grapes* for a Guinness and a rest, and 'Me dad liked his tot of brandy too'.

But the winters got harsher, and over the years less people asked for buttonholes – 'They went to proper florists instead y'see,' – and it was wicked outside the station as the wind lashed her full in the face, making it like parchment. Wicked the winters and the rainy summers, with her wet headscarf clinging to her hair.

Her jet black hair, which curled its way down over her shoulders, is white now, but the rings, the jewellery remain, a marcasite, a sovereign, a cameo.

Gradually she began to bend and fall, gradually even her bones began to ache, and after seasons of standing at the hospital, the station, the cemetery where her mam's buried, she knew that she couldn't take any more merciless English weather.

'After Christmas I'll jack it in,' she'd say. Then with a spell of warm weather she'd break her resoltuion, until now she was too old to carry on.

She slipped into the system of the hospital so well, that after a time she was no longer aware of it. She could still call into *The Grapes* on a Saturday afternoon for a quick one, still laugh, still talk even though, 'I'm not too good on me pins,' even though, as she passed her old selling pitches, she'd think, 'I don't half miss me mam.' If she grieved, she grieved privately. If she ever cried, no one saw her. When she placed herself in care, it was for companionship, and trips to Blackpool to see The Lights, and a sing-song on the coach coming home.

Annie did not cry out.

Annie Gaffney had her memories – and her indomitable spirit.

SCHEDULE ONE:–

WARD PROCEDURE:–

6-00 am	Patients awakened, washed and sat up in bed. Given a cup of tea.
7-30 am	Breakfast served. After breakfast days work commences. Patients who are able are dressed and taken to the dayroom. Any who are due to be bathed are cared for next. Patients who are too ill to get up, or who are bed-ridden, are given a bed bath and all the pressure areas cared for. (Pressure areas are those places where the bones are near to the surface of the skin on which patients lie, i.e. shoulder blades, elbows, knees, heels.) All bedridden patients have their pressure areas seen to every time you do a bed round, or have to change their bed clothes owing to incontinence.

My flesh and my skin he hath made old;
He hath broken my bones.

10-30 to	
11-30 am	Mid morning patients have a milky drink.
12-00 Noon.	Lunch served. Then there is another bed round for the bedridden. Those patients who are in the day room are taken to the toilet.
3-00 pm.	Afternoon tea.
5-00 to	
6-00 pm	Supper. Start to put the patients back to bed.
8-00 pm	Day staff finish duty. Night staff commence duty. Patients are given another milky drink, then settled down for the night. Final bed round.

He hath set me in dark places,
as they that be dead.

SCHEDULE TWO:—

GENERAL NOTES:—

When first admitted, patients are examined by the doctor on duty. (In a geriatric ward the consultant makes only one round per week, but there is usually a house doctor on call in case of an emergency). The duty doctor will order any tests he thinks are necessary, and will probably ask for urine and blood samples to be taken. (Such samples are required from patients on any ward, not just geriatric). Doctor will then prescribe drugs, sleeping tablets or any other medicines necessary and will enter the prescription on that patients *Drug Card*. Medicines are administered at 10-00 am, 2-00 pm, 6-00 pm and 10-00 pm.

Not everybody has medication four times a day. This is, of course, dependent on several factors, such as : (1) the disease the patient is suffering from, (2) the drugs which the patient is already receiving and (3) the dosages already prescribed by doctor, etc.

When I cry out,
He shutteth out my prayer.

GENERAL NOTES:-

Blood pressure is always taken when medicines are administered. On every ward there is a *Kardex* system in which every patient is listed.
Observations (including special observations) by the day and night staff are recorded in the *Kardex*, so that there is an AM-PM report on every patient, every day that they are in care.

And I said,
my hope and my strength is perished from the Lord.

APPENDIX A:-

A patient who cannot swallow or who is unconcious is given a liquid diet consisting of egg and milk, *Complan* and tea, *Bovril* or water. This 'meal' is administered by means of a *Ryles Tube*. This is a thin rubber tube having an olive pointed extremity. It is inserted up the nose and passed down into the stomach.
THESE PATIENTS IF INCONTINENT ARE CATHETERIZED.
A catheter is a tubular, flexibile, surgical instrument for withdrawing fluids from, or

introducing them into, a cavity of the body. Especially one for introducing into the bladder through the urethra, for the withdrawal of urine into an external container, (usually a polythene bag with fluid markings on it), which is changed when full. Patients who can feed themselves will, of course, use bedpans or commodes. All patients are put on '*Intake*' and '*Output*' charts in order to see how well their kidneys are, or are not, functioning. See EXAMPLE ONE . . .

Come hence, do not tarry

Mummy I'm frightened of the dark! Mummy where are you? Oh where are you mummy? Mummy where have you gone?

Cries for help, these noises don't reach the upper floors or, rather, only fragments get that far. For those in Poplar Ward on the third floor hear only the very ends of the sounds, those in Poplar hear only the tail end of life. Here is the last resting place, here is the doorway to Eternity.

The one thing, the only thing which strikes you about this small, tall, tiled room is its silence, its utter stillness. And in four beds, four people lie swathed in blankets and age. Three women, one man. Although now their sex is merely academic. They seem unbelievably small, and as fragile as porcelain, lying there staring or snoozing under sedation, letting the odd word form then drop from their lands of enchantment.

Through the fire-escape door in one corner of the room a single tree can be seen waving extravagantly, swishing. When one of the four dies, he or she will be wrapped in a single red blanket, slung over a shoulder, then taken through the fire-escape door (which overlooks a racecourse), and into an ambulance which will take them to the mortuary. This way, the other patients aren't upset. The red blanket is always kept close by. It is used regularly.

This is the ward which has the most male nurses on it, and there's a story among these men that during your first week on Poplar, the masturbation ratio soars. There's something chilling in the way the nurses on this ward behave. Not exactly aloof, but vaguely embarrassed, vaguely guilty. And that *awful* red blanket! They clatter around in sensible shoes, and the new female nurses stop short, listening, realising how loud their footfalls seem. Occasionally a bed is smoothed, a pillow lifted, an old head placed back into sumptuous white down.

The trees beating wildly against the fire-escape.

Give me your hand my Snow Princess. And I will take you to the hall of the Mountain King. To where the swans are beautiful. To where the Fairy King and Queen lie in flowers. To the Land of Enchantment. To where all the colours are young.

In their beds they seem to lie full fathoms five. Smiling to the air, cursing the humiliations of the bedpan. Now, almost objects, self-respect has withered away or rather reveals itself in shreds, in the closing of the eyes, or in an aristocratic, indifferent stare at the ceiling as the ancient penis cowers under the flannel, or the vast drawers are pulled down from the old-smelling hips to prevent bed-sores.

'There we are dear,' with that awful forced jollity of the embarrassed, or 'Come *along* dear,' when, now and again, one of these four somehow, from somewhere, manages to summon up enough courage to protest against these outrages.

But youth always wins. Strength is always *the* deciding

factor. The weak must perish, go to the wall so that the S.R.Ns shall inherit the earth.

Nothing happens in Poplar except death.

There is no future here, only history. There is no today, only yesterday. There is no peace, only struggle. There is no hope, only survival. For Poplar is the end of the road, the final watershed.

On some high, bright day, their number will be depleted. On that day, the red blanket will be used. So too the fire-escape door.

Then, after a while, their number will be brought back up to strength.

Yet the shock-waves will ricochet for days, weeks, as they dimly realise that the next cough might be their last, that this is the final showdown, the reward or retribution; or, more simply, the monolithic, numbing fear which will dictate how you will die. With courage? Perhaps. With dignity? Perhaps not. When it comes – the death rattle and the fluttering tongues and the choking disbelief in your own mortality – against this, the stature of man telescopes down to infinite smallness, like the clapping of a pair of hands in an empty theatre, like laughter down a well.

Yet in this temple stillness there is life – just. Flickering away like small red candles on side altars.

Through the window in the fire-escape door you can watch nature beating against the glass howling for vengeance. Yet inside, these frail, fragile people blink away the days, settle down in warmth, casting minds back, never forward, to finality and the embrace by fire. When that thought creeps softly in, the flesh tightens, the blood runs cold and there is no comfort.

And so in this house of years, this charnel house where the memories of wise men linger in the Reign of Victoria, where the women tell stories of life below stairs in the '90s, life is coming to a conclusion.

But don't be afraid. Don't be afraid. Mortality is nothing to be frightened of. If you think of it as simply 'not being'. In the abstract. It might be easier. It isn't you in that coffin, in that hearse, in that church painted and decked with flowers under the mosaiced faces of the perfect dead. No it isn't *you* . . . It isn't anyone . . . they simply don't put someone in a box and bury them . . . they . . . just . . . *don't*.

And so we live – through the long, sad days; through the clean, cold nights. Live only in the knowledge of the past, and believe only in its certainty, because our pasts stretch back into infinity.

Here there is no future, only the finite present.

Here there is only the glimmer of life.

Looking out through the window a strong wind in an empty sky. And a steady rain has begun to fall. High winds and rain beating at the window.

Patches of light go off, one-by-one, until there are no more lights left to be extinguished.

Must rest, must get some sleep.

The gas fire on the wall hissing gently, the odd sigh, the old yawn, the stillness, the silent drooping of heads, the quiet ecstasy.

The lagoon, the sky, summertime, fishing and sleeping on banks, the banks of rivers. And grass, dreaming in swaying grass, insects droning and buzzing in ears, traffic humming in the middle distance. The waking sleep, luxurious and swimming in seas of blue skies and clouds like white of egg, mere puffs of nothing, drifting aimlessly in an aimless sky on a summers afternoon. Another lifetime on another planet, the apex of perfection.

Yet here in the falling darkness, in this warm, unnatural dark, the heads ease back into the pillows, disappear into deserts of white, Irish linen, smelling of ether and efficient laundry methods. The mouths fall open, an eiderdown is pulled closer, a hand trembles. A cough. A tear. Not a sound.

As on we sleep.

6-00 am.

It's still dark. The radiators glow, warm and dark, womb-like. Voices and toast.

In come the nurses, cold in clusters, tired-eyed, cloaked, with icing on their hair. Morning, and the dark seeping away under the gathering light, and the birds – a solitary chirp heard at first light, then gradually whole choirs of birds, on this day, late in December.

'Morning staff.'

'Morning girls.' Round faced and jolly in blue.

Trolleys bang far off down corridors, someone sings then whistles, lengthy coughing, dust in the empty dispensary, silent radiography.

It begins to get lighter. A crisp, yellow light falling in through the windows, as the suburban traffic hums towards town.

And slowly the hospital stirs itself into life, as more and more people bang and shout down the long, tiled hallways, clashing aluminium lids, slow cleaners sing as they polish red floors, working their way down towards physiotherapy.

Activity, and the smell of toast in the room adjacent to Poplar – just off the upper corridor.

'How's Miss Jordan today?'

'Wakie-wakie Annie!'

'How's Rosie then?'

'Ups a daisy Pop.'

Always the same, always cheerful in this winter crispness. Red fingered, they lift me up and begin to rub and probe and remove the nightly soiled bed clothes, replacing the rubber undersheet with a, 'What are we going to do with you, Pop?' And my breath catching as their cold hands roam over my inert body, like twenty icicles. And the nurses always smelling like that of ether and eau-de-cologne.

Gradually Poplar comes alive.

Annie is rubbed, then rocks herself from side to side into a sitting position, in order to drink her tea.

Miss Jordan quivering inside her woollen bed jacket, her failing eyes squinting through tears towards her cupboard, her long, frail arms search for the cup, then, finding it, slowly, with great dignity, guiding it towards her lips.

Ancient-headed Rosie struggles into a sitting position, her head bowed, her mouth slack, her chin sunk, lolling towards her pendulous breasts. She lumbers towards her tea with both hands shaking violently. In the painful journey from saucer to mouth, she remembers that her slide is not in her hair, without drinking she replaces the cup with the greatest difficulty, then begins clumsily to search for it with shaking, uncontrollable hands fumbling in the bedclothes. Just the eyes moving, the saliva falling, but her head permenantly bowed onto her chest.

'Here it is dear,' says the nurse as she often does, and cruelly slips the slide into Rosie's scant, grey hair, so that it's pudding cut is now exaggerated by the tortoise-shell slide clipped thoughtlessly over her left ear, making her look like an abnormal, grotesque schoolgirl.

She smiles, then is still, then remembers her tea. And the long, quivering journey towards it begins once more, but it's lukewarm by now, and too milky. They never know how to make a decent cup of tea in here . . .

PARKINSONS DISEASE:– PARKINSONISM:–A group of neurological disorders characterised by hypokinesia (abnormally decreased mobility), tremor and muscular rigidity.

All the world shakes, from head to foot, and the saucer is always too far away. Isn't it Rosie? My Posie?

PARKINSONS SYNDROME:– A form of PARKINSONISM due to idiopathic degeneration of the corpus striatum or substantia nigra, frequently occurring as a sequel to lethargic encephalitis, although cerebral arterioschlerosis, toxins, neurosyphilis and trauma have also been implicated. It is chacterterized by muscular rigidity, immobile facies (Parkinson's Facies), slow, involuntary tremor (present at rest, but tending to disappear during sleep or volitional movement), abolition of associated automatic movements, festinating gait, stooped posture, and salivation. Called also POSTENCEPHALITIC PARKINSONISM. THIS IS A PROGRESSIVE DISEASE.

7.30am.

In a while, breakfast. In a while, another day waiting to be filled. In a while the nurses will be active.

The breakfast trolley with the soft wheels purrs into the ward.

Annie is hungry, Miss Jordan peckish. Pop has to be fed by Ryles Tube. Rosie will need help, as she eats by force of habit in her permanent, broken 'S' position. It is difficult to know whether she feels hunger or sorrow or pain – she just seems to follow nature and the habits of a lifetime. As she keeps her long vow of silence, as it is time to eat, time to defecate, time to lie down, time to sit up, with never a suggestion that her interior world is anything but utterly decayed.

BLOOD PRESSURE:– Indifferent.
TEMPERATURE:– Indifferent.
PULSE:– Slow

But surfaces can be deceptive, can't they, my posie?

Breakfast over, once dressed, Annie waddles towards the dayroom, where she can sit and snooze. Pop and Miss Jordan, bed ridden, wait and dread the coming humiliations. And Rosie – bent double, trembling towards the light, crippled by Parkinsons Disease – makes the long, slow journey from the sheets to the chair which is between her bed and the outer wall.

Sitting there she can remember a time when she was young, before she was married, before the First World War, and Tommy's favourite song . . . *Meet me tonight in dreamland* . . . as he stood rocking on his artificial legs in the kitchen. His legs were shot to pieces in a field, near a river, somewhere in Belgium. Standing by the cooker, gasping for breath, bending down to tie his shoelaces . . . *Meet me in dreamland, dreamy-dreamy dreamland. There let my dreams come true* . . . his frail no-longer-young voice singing in the late afternoon.

Tom who loved Chrysanths. Tom who fought at Vimy Ridge and who was gassed. Passchendaele, The Somme, occasionally seeing French or Haig in their field uniforms – smart and crisp – these phlegmatic men who conducted the slaughter (with aplomb) from warm G.H.Qs far from the mud; these men who hadn't fought a battle since Waterloo.

Ypres, 1915, with the first sniff of German gas hanging green above the trenches. And years later his lungs as stiff as leather, as he snatched for air by the seaside.

All those years ago, brass bands in the park playing brisk marches by Stamford or Elgar, Blackpool in the '30s, tins of cocoa, breadlining, Jarrow, contained poverty, and a King who abdicated for the love of a woman.

Instinctively, Miss Jordan crosses her arms across her chest X-wise, in a small gesture of modesty, her hands clinging to her thin shoulders as they are pulled down away from her, as she is denuded. 'This is hateful! How can they be so brutal? Don't wipe my bum! Don't wipe my bum!'

But no use, no use.

As she is washed, then redressed.

Eggs, milk, tea, water, pass quietly down the Ryles Tube, into his stomach. Funny not to taste your food, as another nurse changes the bag on the side of the bed which has filled during the night, seeping quietly out through the penis, through rubber into a transparent bag. Funny not feeling anything when you pee.

It hurt when they put it into me. It hurt!

And the smell, the constant taste of rubber on everything I swallow, as it glides silently into my stomach.

And now they've started their fucking rubbing! Shoulders, elbows, knees, heels. Every day, always at the same time. I smell of piss and ointment and I *long* for scented soap.

The light gets stronger, the day inches towards 11 o'clock. Milk today. Sometimes it's egg and milk. Or *Horlicks*.

In clusters at the foot of each bed – doctor, sister, two nurses. Nothing showing on their immobile faces, as they scan the charts hanging at the foot of each bed. White fingered, white coated, lean, intelligent, practical people, running through data, sifting symptoms, quietly exchanging questions and answers, just below the breath.

The group dissolves, trickles across the floor, then collects around another bed and the ritual continues like some solemn, almost courtly dance. When doctor makes his once-a-week round, everything hangs suspended. Counterpanes are brushed down to remove wrinkles. Linoleum gleams – ridden of dust. Discipline springs into the air like Aldershot, and sister (looking worried) comes in and glances anxiously around the ward in case anything, in case some displaced object, should offend the doctor. And when it has passed her inspection a reverential, anticipatory hush falls, as they all hover expectantly outside Poplar waiting for a doctor as sister tapping lightly on the filing cabinet.

Then in he comes.

Zadok the priest and Nathan the prophet.

Doctor's natal hands disappear into the pockets of his white coat, along with his pen and his folded stethoscope, as he dreams of a consultancy and the paradise of private practice. He takes a chart, scans it, looks at the patient (so lost in age), then gives it to sister, who hands it to staff nurse, who hands it to the trainee nurse, who clips it back onto the bedrail.

And above cherubim – seraphim.

His round complete, he smiles wryly at sister, then minuets away – for a chat in casualty.

Noon.

And the yellow morning light fading towards afternoon. The wind getting up, as it whistles through the tree outside, which is like joined hands praying.

Annie goes to the toilet.

Miss Jordan prim on the commode.

Pop – lost in the wastes of paralysis – is still.

Rosie sits in her chair at one end of the ward, smiling, sitting as still as her limbs allow, occasionally touching her hair, occasionally running her tongue over her teeth, trying to catch the saliva. And all around her, the lingering smell of pear-drops.

One day she won't shake anymore. One day all will be calm, all will be still. One day she will flicker out on a wave of silence. No more struggle, no point, no need.

The floral screen will quiver around her bed, and at last her head – no longer bowed – will ease back, will touch the pillow and, at last, she will lie straight, for the first time in twenty years as someone – from wards away – whistles selections from the Rogers and Hart song book.

Lunch.

Then the long, long wait till tea.

The light grows heavier, the wind drops.

Laughing from sister's room, the clinking of tea cups, crisp biscuits snapped in half. Crumbs, rumpled uniforms, thermometers, girls sitting down to take the weight off their chests. Cool linoleum, porcelain, shoes creaking step by step past Poplar, drowsy and languid in the late afternoon.

A dark, darkening sky. Weak evening sunlight sinking down to grey, then back to yellow as the clouds pass, white and black, across the sky. A strong wind blowing from the south east making the shrubbery shudder to one side. Spasmodic rain and wet windows. Then the frantic rush of leaves across the roof, scratching the window panes. The iron fire escape rattling, dripping in the damp, chilly air. The clouds disperse, leaving a pale blue sky which flushes pink, then purple, then vermillion, then gold. And night begins to fall.

5.30 pm.

Supper and back to bed.

Annie from the day-room.

Miss Jordan from her upright position.

Pop horizontal.

Rosie trekking.

SENILITY:– The sum of the phsyical and mental deterioration occurring in old age.

Six. Seven. Eight o'clock. A nice cup of tea. New faces arrive, old faces remain. Bedding them down for the night.

'Goodnight Pop.'

'Ni-Nite Rosie.'

'Sleep tight Miss Jordan.'

'Pleasant dreams Annie.'

The dark. The final bed round. The lone torch shone on four faces. Her black shoes. Her cloak. As she sits under a small light at the end of the ward, or goes to sister's room to sigh or drink at midnight.

They slide into sleep.

Silence. Utter calm. The long day is over.

Sheep may safely graze.

Christmas.

A parable, a parable.

Hello Pop.

Miss Jordan.

Rosie.

Annie.

Oh Pop, Pop. Don't you remember the snow and the tinsel and your new green suit – your first with *long* trousers. And snowballs, and tissue-covered fruit along the side-board, walnuts milky in the mouth, and the teeming presents glittering in the firelight. But most of all, the melting snow drifts mounting high against the railings, sliding down from roof tops to the street. Icicles on the backyard wall.

Steel-grey cloud massing over the whole town and, during the night, the gentle snowflakes massing in the areas up against the window panes, floating down the silent chimney, melting on the coals, covering the world – a silent, white land.

Tony bringing chocolate and raisins, John and Kevin scattering snow from along the window ledge, from off the parapit railings, then hurling it like powder over each other.

Eileen, Maisie, Helen, picking their way, in high heels, through rivers of melting snow. Stepping into bigger footprints made earlier by bigger, phantom men. Wet nylons, pinched toes inside patent leather, tide marks just above the sole. Breath hanging in the air, masking the face.

Mum cooking (for hours on end), the yearly leg of pork, sage and onion fingers, her smile and her staying up all night to do the housework, making everywhere look radiant for Christmas Day. Then with the pork sizzling in the oven, the house quiet, her children in bed – her solitary pilgrimage to midnight mass with her leather purse open, ready for the priests' silver collection . . .

And it came to pass that a decree went out from Caesar Augustus that all the world should be taxed.

. . . and pagan the pomp of mass shining before the high altar as the Eucharist – held with the thumb and forefingers of the priest – is raised up, and in unison the faithful sinking to their knees, bowed heads, the muttered prayer calling for mercy from the white disk, *Mea culpa, mea culpa, mea maxima culpa!* With her gentle fist gently beating her chest, just above the heart . . . *Through my fault, through my fault, through my most grevious fault!* As if *she* had anything to confess, this faultless woman . . . Transubstantiation . . . The Body and Blood of Christ held in a cup, resting on a paton, caught in a vessel of gold, the chasuble and the alb, the chalice, weak altar wine, and the divine crumbs carefully eaten, carefully mingled with the wine, then drunk. . .

This is My Body and My Blood

. . . and white and gold the vestments and the Glory of God, The Son of Man, shepherds abiding in the fields, watching their flocks. . .

Oh come all ye faithful,
Have another plateful.

Blessed art thou amongst women. As she takes out her silver, lets it fall on to the green felt of the collecting plate.

Ite missa est

Go – the mass is ended. In a blaze of light, in an ecstasy of orthodoxy.

Do this in commemoration of me.

Then she shuffles home to the spitting meat, through the snow, with a fine powder crisp underfoot, and God is in her pocket.

A parable, a parable.
Oh Miss Jordan . . . Miss Jordan, don't you remember the singing of the choir? And the school play, depicting The Flight into Egypt, and angels with quivering halos five inches

above the head. *We Three Kings of Orient are*, bearing gifts. Cotton snow on the window ledge in S4, the bottles of red ink, the bookcases bought by the army of school children you taught, and prayers with the eyes shut, and the love of God, and the children making Christmas cards for their parents, staring with awe, in holy silence, at the school crib as if those little, painted figures standing there so blandly amongst the straw were really sacred.

> *O Star of wonder, star of night,*
> *Guide us with they perfect light.*

Do you remember Miss Jordan? Do you?

A parable, a parable.
Do you remember all your Christmases together with Tommy? Always the same answer – 'We had a good time – quiet but nice,' – and the front room buoyant with self-conscious decorations. In the form of a star – crêpe on the dusty ceiling, and the fruit bowls filled, 'A pound of oranges, a pound of apples, two pound of tangerines – Tommy likes a tangerine – and a box of dates for meself,' regularly, every year. And a card for Tommy, and he sneaks out to get one for her. And small gifts, clumsily wrapped, which are the same year after year – socks for him, shortbread for her. Oh do you remember Rosie? My Posie?

A parable, a parable
Annie bathed in flowers. Can you forget Annie? And more fruit than you'd ever seen, stacked in the parlour, waiting to be resold. Then getting out early to catch the trade in town, shouting, pushing your flowers in a keen, bitter wind, with the snowflakes sticking to the head and eyelashes, numbing your fingers until you couldn't give change. The notes sticking together, needing to be blown apart on the wet,

wet, multi-coloured paving stones, under the weak, orange street lighting. The heavy traffic, the big wicker basket, aching feet and limbs and a cuppa waiting for you when you got home, as you counted your takings, adding it to your mam's to make a record year – with your dad gloomy over the fire, this being his twelfth year out of a job. Kids snow shifting, knocking at the front door, and you always gave them a wet two bob piece and a handful of nuts or a bag of apples. 'Merry Christmas Missus!' as they gasp away, icy-handed, blowing on red fingers, arguing over who gets first choice.

All the Christmases ever lived are here in this tiny room. The wet shoes and leaking galoshes. The cherished cards and joyous laughter. The grotto and the king. The carols and the adoration. The Saviour and the saved. *Bearing gifts we travel so far – Guide us to thy perfect light*. The memories that have sustained them for so long can still work their magic, if only a little.

Oh my babies! My little ones!

The small Thai nurse giggles as she inflates balloons. Decorations in loops, softening the white ward, the hardness of tiles. And miraculously, from somewhere, someone brings a small, blue, artificial tree (with artificial snow) hung with small, inexpensive gifts – a pen, a brooch, some butterscotch, and a bottle of scent.

They've tried to make the ward look pretty for Christmas.

> *And the angel of the Lord shone about them and they were sore afraid.*

Miss Jordan is all stone.

ENDOGENOUS HYPOTHERMIA:– Abnormally reduced body temperature resulting from physiological causes, due to dysfunction of the central nervous system of the endocrine system.

Oh Miss Jordan, you're *so still*, lying there as your temperature drops to below sub normal and your pulse rate skips quietly towards a hundred a minute as the pains in your chest get worse and inflammation spreads, in patches, all over the lungs, as you slip quietly into unconsciousness. . .

PNEUMONIA – INFLUENZAL PNEUMONIA – INFLUENZAL VIRUS PNEUMONIA:– A severe, usually fatal disease, caused by influenza virus, and characterized by abrupt onset, high fever, prostration, sore throat, aching pains, profound dyspnea and anxiety, and by massive pulmonary haemorrhagic edema and consolidation. It may be complicated by BACTERIAL PNEUMONIA, in which case the symptoms of that disease (shaking chills, pleuritic pains, etc) are superimposed on the PRIMARY INFLUENZA VIRUS PNEUMONIA. HYPOTHERMIA IS LINKED WITH THIS DISEASE.

. . . from somewhere she can hear – oh ever so faintly – a Salvation Army band, getting fainter and fainter all the time, playing, playing. *Christ was born in Beth-le-hem*, *Silent Night*, *Adeste Fidelis*, *Away in a manger*. Softer than soft now, warm dark notes on the brass, the halo of light, the glittering school play, the processions. The boys fresh faced on Confirmation Day, glowing in candles. Their first confession, their first Holy Communion in white ringlets, pearl-coloured prayer books and your first set of rosary beads – white – and blessed by a cardinal. The long dedication of a working life – stubbornly reading Milton, forcing them to listen to *Fingals Cave* or *Blow the Winds Southerly*, Shakespeare, and patriotism on Empire Day, trying to explain *Wuthering Heights* to the under-12s. Playing the piano for the last lesson on the last school day. And all are here, Miss Jordan, to say 'goodbye'. *Way down upon the Swanee River*, *Whistling Rufus the one-man band*. Negro spirituals. Miss Jordan liked negro spirituals, and Stephen Foster, and Geoffrey Whitby's eyelashes, *Swing low sweet charri-ot*. And all the children she has ever taught are crowded into the room and about her bed – like a last pageant, and they kiss her hands, and their letters cascade around her in a golden shower, and they all are singing just for *her*. . .

Away in a-a manager, No-o crib for a bed,
The-e litt-tle Lord Jesus lay-ay down his sweet head

. . . Dying away . . . softer and softer . . .

A-and stay by my bedside ti-il morning is nigh

TEMPERATURE:– High.
BLOOD PRESSURE:– High.
PULSE RATE:– Fast.

. . . at last all her ghosts leave her, at last she is engulfed by the golden glory of her 10,000 children – leaving only this outer shell, leaving this Miss Jordan – in her lonely durability, in her indestructible pride, in her granite self-possession – far, far behind.

At 5-15 on Christmas Eve – just as dusk was falling – Miss Jordan died.

'Ups a daisy Pop.'
'How'd you like to sit up today?'
As they raise the bed rest, I slowly rise into a semi-upright position.
'There you go!'
Why all the fuss?
Why all the special attention?
They adjust the bed rest, wash my face, comb my hair.
Why all this activity?
I can look around in *real* comfort now.
Annie, for the first time ever during the day, is lying coughing in bed and rubbing her heart, just below the breast.

Miss Jordan's empty bed.
Rosie's crippled, dozing in a chair.
Perhaps I'm to have? . . .
No, no. It isn't possible. . .

From his bed he can see out through the ward door leading to the main corridor, which passes Poplar at right angles. On the left, the dispensary, on the right, sister's room.

D'you think?

The thought drops in from out of the fog.

Perhaps I'm to get visitors? Oh. Oh yes, perhaps I'm to get *visitors!* Tony, and John, and Kevin, Eileen and Maisie and Helen. Oh will they come? Will they? Oh how I *long* to see them!

What's the time?

10-00 am.

It's so early, it'll be such a long wait, but worth it in the end.

And all who pass his bed smile or shout across to him. . .

'You'll be on your feet next.'

'The Pyjama Game!'

11-00 am.

Tea, but I'm too excited to drink it. Delicious sensations run through my stomach and down my left side, as I imagine them around the bed, exchanging jokes, leaving money on the locker, trying to hide their concern, trying to express their love in the smallest of gestures. I know how they will be. I just *know*.

Oh I'm sure to have visitors. I'm just sure to! That's why they've gone to so much trouble to smarten me up. They've never gone to such lengths before.

Noon.

Time hangs, time hangs.

1-00 pm.

And still they don't come. Oh where are they?

They're dead. They died.

My left side stops tingling, as a dread descends. Then unusual chattering is heard – getting closer and closer – and every nerve shivers and vibrates. But the voices drift past, and are gone. And the dull feeling of dread hangs heavier.

Who's this . . .? Is it . . .? What if they don't . . .? What if . . .?

Perhaps they've been given special permission to come at any time. Yes, that's it – I've been so ill that they'll be able to visit me at any time. And all is delight, all is brightness again.

2-00 pm.

3-00 pm.

No, no, it can't be.

4-00 pm.

5-00 pm.

6-00 pm.

The hours running together into evening.

7-00 pm.

8-00 pm.

And as they fail to arrive, a sullen optimism sets in. Familiar footfalls I know to be sister's or staff's, I imagine are different, new. But the footsteps either peter out or stop short of Poplar, then tap away in the same direction as they came.

I know they didn't actually *say* I was going to get visitors, I know that, but everything led me to believe that I would, and I *did want* them so. In my heart I know no one will come now, in my heart I know that no one ever will.

'My! My! What a sour face!' As sister looms past, as she quick-marches off duty.

I knew they wouldn't come. I just knew.

And he begins to cry, screaming out in little jets of confusion.

I wanted then to come.

I did.

I DID.

> *By the rivers of Babylon, there we sat down,*
> *yea, we wept when we remembered Zion.*

'What's all this Pop?'
'Oh we can't have this!'
Staff nurse – practical and impervious to my embarrassing, distorted howling – lowers the bed rest and settles me down for the night.
'Just look at that face! It'd stop a clock.'

> *For there they that carried us away captive,*
> *required of us a song; and they that wasted us*
> *required of us mirth, saying, Sing us one of*
> *the songs of Zion.*

Horizontal again, and something has died in him.
'Come on – give us a smile.'

> *How shall we sing in a strange land?*

And I do so – obediently.

> *O Daughter of Babylon who art to*
> *be destroyed.*

Now all passion is subdued. Now even despair has gone. Only the self – frail, trembling – quivers like ancient glass and allows itself to be stilled or carried or rubbed with oil, by rote, by schedule, by clock.

To be able to fix a point in time and keep it like a treasure. To die young is a blessing – to live to be *so old* – the wrath of God.

Their collective ages number centuries, some of their marriages have lasted fifty years or more, and at the turn of the century, their mothers were young and actually *saw*

Queen Victoria. And she was so *old*.

There was a time (I remember it) when people didn't get old. There was a time when you didn't lock them away. There was a time when, to be old, was to be wise, to be revered, to know secrets that only age brought. But now? They just want to be rid of us, them and their 'nuclear' families.

Here, now, on the edges of the world we totter and balance, as delicately as leaves in air. We wait, we watch, we keep vigil and, yes, we actually *hope*. Behind the sunken eye, below the withered hand, the embers still glow in the dark. The false fire between the legs – that old, old passion – even now, even here one can still feel the faintest stirring – like a stick in dry leaves. When it's hot and that young male nurse comes in sweating and desirable in shadows, with a light film of sweat shimmering on his glowing skin; even now, even here, although the hair is as fine as gold, as brushed as silk, we wait, we count, we are warm, are cold, we inexplicably smile or cry, or stare, or fold our pasts about us like linen cloaks. We feed on bread and milk, or mashed food which is easy to swallow – but most of all we wait. But the days pass, but the days pass. And the hours crawl by like years. The breath fainter. The will to live frailer. Then *blessed* sleep.

In the darkness, between two sighs, the world hangs.

Miss Jordan, gone.
Pop.
Rosie.
Annie.
But what are you thinking Annie? What do you *feel* as you lie there, still as snow? As the blood stream lumbers through your body?

On the wall, the gas-fire humming warmth, crooning memories.

In the pub. Oh don't you remember? In the pub . . . in the pub . . . a sing-song . . . the woman with the dairy-maid face singing *Until the Twelfth of Never* into your eyes, and smiling and telling you that she will love you for a long, *long* time. Christmas cards on the table for Dot and Lil, Dot who was in the land army with another scouse called Betty Christian who was only five foot nothing and six stone, but who could move more manure than anyone else. In the singing, shining face, the experience of a lifetime – but shared. Shared air-raid shelters in 1940 when they rationed energy, and Hitler was still alive, and rhetoric flooded from a Winston Churchill radio, when Lord Haw-Haw made bombing predictions in the inferno of May 1940. In a gentle England, in a time long, long ago, in The Land of Make-Believe and of courage unlimited. And the songs tumble out – *Little Saucepans, Knees Up Mother Brown, I should've Been a Barra-Boy Years Ago, I'm 'Enerry the Eighth I am* as the faces sparkle and shine. 'Merry Christmas' signs just above the till.

And hair . . . grey hair, a shock of hair, purplish skin, pudding hands with swollen fingers, short, crusty nails flecked with black, fingers resembling bloated sausages.

He nods to her – this man – in his ailing, purple fifties but doesn't speak. He offers her the tea-pot and winks, drinks his soup, eats his meal, his dessert. Then rolls a cigarette in his Irish hands, lingers over his tea cup then says, ' I'll go down to the pub later.' But you're dead dad . . . dad, you *died*.

Then his strong, Irish voice comes sailing over the rooftops, as he comes singing home, his eyes full, his boots, his tight grey suit, his cap. And Annie on the landing, squinting through the bannisters, and wishing 'Can I come down Dad?' As he would come clambering into the house, smelling like a barrel, shouting for his tea and pea soup, flushed, weepy and homesick for Ireland – that martyred land. Then, he would stop, pause, and looking into the lentils, softly begin to sing . . .

Just a lad of eighteen summers . . .

'Sing *Kevin Barry*, Dad,' Annie would whisper on the stairs. 'Sing *Kevin Barry*' . . .

He held his noble head high . . .

And his voice, barely audible, but softer than mist, would creep out from under the back kitchen door.

*Kevin Barry gave his young life,
For the cause of Free Ireland . . .*

And every time Kevin marched to the scaffold, he took Annie with him, in tears, from the landing . . .

*All around that little bakery,
We fought the British hand-to-hand . . .*

Oh dad! Dad!

CYANOSIS:– Blueness of face. Pain in chest. Cough (blood stained). Difficult breathing.

*Shoot me like an Irish soldier,
Do not hang me like a dog . . .*

BLOOD PRESSURE:– High.
TEMPERATURE:– High.
PULSE RATE:– Fast.

And her small, stout mother who had sold everything – fruit in the '30s, second-hand baby goods, wood, fire irons, marly horses in chipped china, footwear, braces, Irish linen hankies then finally flowers. Who ran a tontine during the war and who, despite her soft heart, had made a small, stout profit, which she'd put into horticulture. She had been quiet, well-liked, hard-working and shrewd.

'Me mam died first, then not long after, me dad.'

PULMONARY EMBOLISM:– The sudden blocking of an artery by a clot of foreign material which has been brought to its place of lodgement by the blood stream.

Mam me hands are cold! . . . Oh.
Mam me hands are *so cold*! . . . Oh.
Mam . . . Mam . . .
A short, convulsive jerk, a look of surprise and shock, then her plump, rotund body lay still.
Quietly, without fuss, Annie Gaffney died.
An embolism during the night.
The night staff change, the day staff come and go . . .
Rosie.
Pop.
Miss Jordon.
Herself.
Dappled skin so soft, so cared for now, with the world turning, with the heart empty . . .

> *Until the twelfth of never,*
> *And that's a long, long time . . .*

The Time is at hand.

> *At the round earth's imagin'd corners, blow*
> *Your trumpets, angells, and arise, arise*
> *From death, you numberless infinities*
> *Of soules, and to your scattred bodies goe.*

Alas, alas that city Babylon, that mighty city! Thy

Judgement is come.

> *Behold he cometh with clouds and His*
> *eyes were as a flame of fire,*
> *And out of His mouth went a*
> *sharp two-edged sword, and He*
> *was clothed in a vesture*
> *dipped in blood.*

Rooks cawing far over to the west – falling hair – and there are edges to the world . . . I thought . . . oh . . . so long ago, that somehow everything would sort itself out, that there would be a resolution to all this . . . but that was all *so long ago* . . .

CEREBRAL THROMBOSIS – STROKE – STROKE SYNDROME:– A condition of sudden onset, caused by acute vascular lesions of the brain, such as haemorrhage, embolism, thrombosis, or rupturing aneurysm; which may be marked by hemiplegia, or hemiparesis, vertigo, numbness, aphasia and dysarthria. It is often followed by permanent neurological damage and/or death.

If only you could grow invisible . . . fade away . . . slip into a gentle dissolution . . . back to God's country . . . or so they say . . . but its all so passive as we rock in boredom and wait . . .

GLOSSARY:–

THROMBOSIS:–	The clotting of blood.
ANEURYSM:–	A weak point in an artery.
HEMIPLEGIA:–	Paralysis of one side of the body.
HEMIPARESIS:–	Incomplete paralysis of one side of the body.
VERTIGO:–	A sense of rotation.

APHASIA:–　　　　　　Inability to express or understand the spoken word. See also GLOBAL APHASIA.

DYSARTHRIA:–　　　　Difficulty in articulation.

And oh! . . . it's hot . . . so hot . . .

BLOOD PRESSURE:–　130 over 90, and rising.

If only I could move it wouldn't be so bad . . .
What time is it?
Sleep away the days . . . I just want to sleep away the days . . . and get it over with . . . and say goodbye . . .

PULSE RATE:–　Weakening. Very rapid.

Clouds have broken and the sun is shimmering on the bed clothes, making them smell peculiar and different today.

RESPIRATION:–　Erratic.

The world flickers once, twice . . . and is still for a moment. And oh, oh a feeling of faintness and nausea washes over me from the hairline to the feet, all on one side. The ward quivers and is insubtantial, then the feeling passes, as joy suffuses the whole body. Relief and weakness . . . nurses faintly around the bed . . . and the calling birds . . .

> *And I looked, and behold a pale horse;*
> *And his name that sat on him was death.*

. . . stay with me staff, sit by me and give me your hand . . .

'They know when they're dying – you go and sit by them – but they know they're going.'

My right side is completely paralyzed, the skin discoloured – purple – the colour of pain. I've tried to speak, but it's too difficult now. So I just lie here and am kept alive. I've tried counting to pass away the time, but I never keep it up . . . anything really . . . OH! . . . OH! I CAN'T SEE THE CEILING! YES, YES, IT'S STILL THERE . . . AND I *burn* all over 2, 3, 4, anything to pass away the time 6, 7, All good children go to heaven 9, 10, anything to get through 12. 13.

CEREBRAL THROMBOSIS:–
TEMPERATURE:–	High.
BLOOD PRESSURE:–	High.
PULSE RATE:–	Fast.

There is a deep coma with dilation of pupils. Difficult breathing which changes to CHEYNE STOKES variety.

The ceiling, the patches of damp, the orange light fitting, the bulb gently swaying . . . it all bends and falls – refracted – as if under water, and I can't see it anymore. It dissolves away, swaying down into blackness as the head explodes, saturating the brain with warm, destructive blood. Bathed in pain. Gently going under for the last time, like a ship at sea.

'If a patient goes on you during the night – don't panic. It's the first sign of incompetence. Put the screens around the bed, strip and wash the patient, then call for a porter. He'll probably bring a trolley, but just to be on the safe side, utilize the one outside sister's room.'

CHEYNE STOKES:– Breathing which occurs in cerebral thrombosis. The long loops represent deep breaths getting shallower; the line is when the breathing has ceased. When the line is continuous – that is the moment of death. The symptoms given are for those patients quite close to death.

Bobbing on tiny waves . . . short – sharp – gasps – hot, rapid eyelids on a flickering sky . . . at last mummy . . . going home . . .

> *The time is at hand.*
> *I am alpha and omega.*
> *I am the resurrection and the life.*
> *The time is at hand . . .*

> Mummy.
> Mummy!
> Where are you mummy?
> Mummy where have you gone?
> Mummy it's dark in here . . .

Peace.
The limousine is long (much longer than a Jaguar which is resembles), low and blue with chrome-edged, removable panels.
Peace.
The body is in the limousine, so that it entirely fills the cavity – snug. Snug.
Peace?
The hall is big like a mock-Tudor ante-chamber, and the faces push and peer down into the casket.

> And from where I'm lying, from my position *inside* the coffin – I can see their faces looking down at me, yet I am unable to speak . . .

The church ceiling. The echoing stillness. Then the lid is screwed on.

>Darkness.
>Silence.
>And the smell of wood in the close, airless, satin-shrouded
>dark . . .

O Pain, O Death.

>And I begin to sweat . . . as the air evaporates . . . as the thin lungs pump, expand, gasp like tissue paper about to burst . . . rapid . . .

Then the lowering into the ground.

>OH CHRIST!

The still, small voice crying in the wilderness.

>OH SWEET JESUS CHRIST!

P E A C E.

>The soil pours down, beating rhythmically against,
>pressing down onto, the screwed-down lid . . .
>Pushing frantically against the long, wooden roof . . .

A voice is heard crying aloud

>LET ME OUT!
>LET ME OUT!

PEACE!

LET ME OOOUUUTTT!

Peace.

NO! ────────────────────────────

And he closes his eyes for the last time
And the room wraps itself around him
And he is afriad to surrender to the final dark

The Last Trumpet.

Babylon the great, is fallen, is fallen.

A FILM TRILOGY BY TERENCE DAVIES
1976-1983

Part 1 CHILDREN (BFI)

The theme is violence—social and domestic—and its effect on the main character Robert Tucker—in Liverpool.

It is told in a series of extended flashbacks—real time occurring roughly in the middle of the film—and reveals incidents from his childhood, his Catholic upbringing and how they have affected his adult life. Constant bullying at school and a violent and sick father at home—all these events affect his sexuality. The film ends with a memory—the death of his father and the boy appears to be trapped in his sexuality and his childhood.

Part 2 MADONNA & CHILD
(National Film & TV School)

A film about the conflict between Catholicism and sexuality.

A severe and intimate portrait of Robert Tucker in middle-age who is trapped between his private and public personae. A dutiful son and conscientious worker, he is also a man for whom religion and sexuality have become synonymous. This dilemma produces in him an overwhelming sense of despair from which he feels there is no escape.

Part 3 DEATH & TRANSFIGURATION
(Greater London Arts Assoc. / BFI)

Part Three completes the story in more ways than being merely the final instalment. It is a summing-up of Tucker's life and his attitude towards the remembered events of his life and of his coming to terms with his own mortality.

In this synthesis of memory, time past and present merge into the single moment which puts into a new perspective Tucker's life and the trilogy as a whole.

At the last, his life is transfigured by the love between him and his mother.

At the last—'There are no sinners, no just... none is great, none is small... simply—we know, we are.'

"impressive... intense... painfully honest."
Philip French, THE OBSERVER

A BFI Release

Available from: Film & Video Library
British Film Institute
81 Dean Street London W1V 6AA
Tel: 01 734 6451